THE STATE'S WITNESS

An Unwanted Dilemma

KYIRIS ASHLEY

URBAN AINT DEAD PRESENTS

URBAN AINT DEAD

P.O Box 960780

Riverdale GA., 30296

Cover Design: Akirecover2cover.com

Edited By: Veronica Rena Miller / Red Diamond Editing by V. Rena, LLC / reddiamondediting5@yahoo.com

Contact Author on FB: Kyiris Ashley / IG: @kyirisashley

Contact Publisher at www.urbanaintdead.com

Email: urbanaintdead@gmail.com

Print ISBN: 979-8-9875422-1-7

Ebook ISBN: 979-8-9875422-2-4

SOUNDTRACK

Scan the QR Code below to listen to the Soundtracks/Singles of some of your favorite U.A.D titles:

Don't have Spotify or Apple Music?
No Sweat!
Visit your choice streaming platform and search URBAN AINT DEAD.

Currently on lock serving a bid?
JPay, iHeartRadio, WHATEVER!
We got you covered.
Simply log into your facility's kiosk or tablet, go to music and search URBAN AINT DEAD.

URBAN AINT DEAD

Like & Follow us on social media:
FB – URBAN AINT DEAD
IG: @urbanaintdead
Twitter: @urbanaintdead
Tik Tok - @urbanaintdead

SUBMISSION GUIDELINES

Submit the first three chapters of your completed manuscript to urbanaintdead@gmail.com, subject line: Your book's title. The manuscript must be in a .doc file and sent as an attachment. The document should be in Times New Roman, double-spaced and in size 12 font. Also, provide your synopsis and full contact information. If sending multiple submissions, they must each be in a separate email. Have a story but no way to submit it electronically? You can still submit to URBAN AINT DEAD. Send in the first three chapters, written or typed, of your completed manuscript to:

URBAN AINT DEAD
P.O Box 960780
Riverdale GA., 30296

DO NOT send the original manuscript. Must be a duplicate.
Provide your synopsis and a cover letter containing your full contact information.

Thanks for considering URBAN AINT DEAD.

CHAPTER ONE

Russell laid back in bed with his legs spread as he looked up at the ceiling. Tianna sat between them with his manhood in her mouth. However, she was taking way too long to make him nut. She didn't know how to suck dick at all, and he knew he would have to give her several lessons before she would be decent at it. In all of his twenty-eight years of life, he'd never had to teach a woman how to suck dick, but for Tianna, he would do so. He liked her vibe and wanted to keep her around. Russell focused his dark brown eyes on the porn that was being played on the fifty-five-inch television in front of him. He bit his bottom lip as he watched the thick, brown skinned woman get pounded from behind. Closing his eyes, he focused on the woman's moans and his dick hardened. Placing his hand on the back of Tianna's head, he pushed it down, causing his dick to go deeper down her throat.

Tianna gagged, forcing more saliva to enter her mouth. Russell grabbed one of her nipples and twirled it between his fingers as he held her head in place. With his eyes still closed, Russell's toes curled as he sensed the feeling of his climax nearing.

"Yes bitch, suck that dick for daddy. Get all that nut outta there," Russell panted, just as he released his warm cum down Tianna's throat.

Tianna sat up and wiped her mouth with her hand. She looked at the way Russell was laid out and breathing heavy, and a smile crossed her face.

"Did I do good, baby?" She asked, eager to hear his answer.

Russell had told her on several occasions that she didn't know how to perform oral sex. She knew that was something Russell really liked, and in order to keep him happy, she wanted to learn the ends and outs. So, she watched porn and searched Goggle in an effort to master the skill of giving head.

"Yeah, that was pretty dope. I'm glad no teeth came out this time. You still have some work to do but you are getting' better," Russell replied.

In reality, Russell wouldn't have came if it wasn't for the porn. He just didn't want to hurt Tianna's pride. He could tell that she really wanted to please him, so he just let her think she had done so.

"I'm gonna get in the shower, I have to work in the mornin'. Are you spendin' the night tonight?" Tianna asked as she stood from the bed.

"Nah, not to night, my baby."

Russell saw the change in Tianna's demeanor and knew she wanted him to stay, but he had money to collect. It was always money over bitches in his eyes. Tianna wasn't making him any money, so he wasn't about to keep wasting his time with her.

"How much you makin' at that little job you got?" Russell asked as he zipped his pants.

"Bout seven hundred every two weeks," Tianna answered confidently.

"What if I tell you I know a way you can double that in just one week, maybe even a few days, dependin' on how good you work?"

"I'm listenin'," Tianna replied.

"You gotta use what you got to get what you want. Has anybody ever told you that as long as you got a pussy, you should never be broke?"

Tianna looked at Russell perplexed. Did this dude just call me broke? I had just swallowed his kids while he moaned like a little bitch, and he has the nerve to stand here and insult me? I may not be big ballin', but I was definitely livin' comfortably. Tianna thought, quickly becoming irritated by the way Russell was talking to her.

"No disrespect, my baby, I'm just tryin' to put you up on game. Let's be real, you been fuckin' and suckin' on me for the last six weeks, for free. I'm sure it's a dozen other niggas that can say that too."

"Are you suggesting that I should fuck for money?" Tianna asked, damn near ready to slap the shit out of Russell.

"Hell yeah, you been givin' it out for free this long. You might as well put a price on that muthafucka."

Russell reached into his pocket and pulled out a wad of money and held it up in Tianna's face, showing her all the bills. He watched as her eyes got wide, and he knew he'd just reeled her in.

"You see this? I made this shit in one week, spreading my knowledge and taking care of girls just like you. You could be makin' this too, just by layin' on yo back or getting' on yo knees. You young and tight, niggas will pay big money for you."

Tianna thought for a minute as she stared at the money in Russell's hand. Money signs started invading her mind, as she thought about all the new things she could buy with the fast money. This could possibly be the lick she was looking for that could change her life forever.

"So, how much you think I can make?" She asked quickly, eagerness in her tone.

Russell looked at her tight, shapely body and short, blonde pixie cut. Tianna stood about five two, with thick hips and ass, and perfect perky C cup breasts. At eighteen with no kids, her body was perfect, and Russell knew the niggas would pay big for her. Although she was black, her butter pecan colored skin and hazel eyes gave her an exotic look, and he knew he could sale that.

"About twelve hundred a week," he replied.

That was a lot of money. Tianna started to do the math in her head. She figured if she worked with Russell for a year, she would be able to purchase her clothing store and become her own boss. It had been her dream for as long as Tianna could remember to own her own boutique. She knew it would take years to save up for it working at McDonald's.

She could save for a decade and still not have enough with the pennies she made there.

"When can I start?" Tianna asked.

Russell smiled because that hadn't taken nearly as much convincing as he thought it would. It was almost too easy, like taking candy from a baby.

"Don't go to work in the mornin'. I'll be back over here in a few hours and we can take some pictures of you to post on my site. After I post them, you should be getting' to work within an hour. That shit don't take long at all."

Tianna nodded her head in understanding, eager to see how the money would start rolling in. She'd never thought she would be selling sex on the internet, but there was no way Tianna could pass up that type of money. Tianna would damn near sale her soul to make enough money to start her own business. Although she didn't realize it, in a way, she was.

"Get you some rest, my baby, you gonna need it, cuz it's gonna be a long night. And that shit smell like money," Russell said, rubbing his hands together while smiling.

Russell walked out the door and Tianna got in bed. She set her alarm for midnight, knowing that Russell would be returning around that time. She fell asleep with money on her mind, feeling as though her hustle was just about to begin.

———

When her clock alarmed at midnight, Tianna rushed to get into the shower. She knew Russell was on his way, and she didn't want to keep him waiting. She quickly showered and rubbed shea butter all over her body before putting on her robe. There was a knock on the door, and she rushed to it, knowing exactly who it was.

"I brought you somethin' sexy to take pictures in," Russell announced. Holding up a red lace pantie and bra set.

Tianna took the lingerie from his hand and went to the bathroom to put them on. She looked at herself in the mirror and knew that a red lip and a set of false lashes would set the look off. She made her way to her vanity and took a seat, ready to complete the look. When she walked back out to the living room with Russell, he smiled at her beauty. Standing to his feet, he removed his phone from his pocket.

Tianna posed several different ways as Russell snapped shot after shot. Russell directed her on different sexier poses for him to snap, telling her to lean against the couch with her leg up. Or squat down with her legs spread and her tongue out. Tianna obliged without protest, doing everything Russell said. When they were done, he picked her four best pictures to post. No sooner than Tianna changed out of the lingerie did Russell tell her she had a date.

"He wants head and pussy, and you gonna make one fifty off the deal," Russell informed.

"Cool, where is this going down at?" Tianna asked.

"We gonna meet him at a room. Go get changed and put on something sexy. Meet me at my truck when you done," Russell spoke, grabbing his keys from Tianna's coffee table.

When they made it to the motel, Russell told Tianna to stay in the car while he went and collected the money. Russell had a strict policy and let all the men know that nothing went down until all the money was in his hand. The man opened the room door and Russell stepped inside. He looked around the room, and in the bathroom, making sure nobody else was inside the room. Russell had only given the john the price for one person and wanted to make sure he wasn't getting played. Once he was sure no one else other than the man was inside, Russell collected four hundred and fifty dollars from him, then walked back out to the car.

"He's ready for you," Russell stated, and Tianna got out of the car.

She walked up to the motel room door and smiled when she saw the man standing on the other side. He was a tall white man who seemed to be in his mid to late forties. He was handsome, with dark brown hair and brown eyes. She could tell he worked out by his washboard stomach. She was happy that he wasn't ugly and fat.

"Hello there," Tianna greeted, as she closed the door behind her.

"Wow, you are absolutely beautiful. What is your name?" He asked.

Tianna though for a moment, cussing herself for not thinking of a name before she got there. Knowing she wasn't going to give her government name; she said the first thing that came to mind.

"You can call me Amber," Tianna replied, as she walked closer to the man.

She slowly began unbuttoning his shirt, revealing his carved chest. Once his shirt was off, she unbuckled his belt and allowed his pants to drop to the floor. She could see his erect manhood standing at attention through his black silk boxers. Tianna was just about to pull them down when he stopped her.

"I paid for you, so let me do this how I want to," He whispered.

Tianna obliged and allowed the man to take control. He pulled Tianna's tight black dress off her and revealed her naked body. The man licked his lips as he stared at Tianna. Bringing her over to the bed, he laid her down and buried his face between her thick thighs. Tianna moaned as the man's wet tongue gave her more pleasure than she'd ever had. When he was done, he placed a condom on his penis and climbed on top of her. Tianna moaned as he entered her.

For this to be her first time on the job, she was really enjoying this. She wasn't nervous at all like she thought she would be. If every time could be just like this, Tianna was going to love her job. Tianna threw it back and popped her pussy like she had known this man for years. When they were done, Tianna was spent. Naked, she walked into the bathroom to wash the sex from her body. When she returned to the room, her john was already fully dressed and sitting on the bed they had just fucked in.

"Here you go, this is for you," he said, handing her two-hundred-dollar bills.

"Oh, I thought you already paid Russell," Tianna said, confused.

"I did, but I really enjoyed myself with you, so this is your tip," he replied with a wink.

Tianna smiled and placed the money in her bra before thanking him. There was no way she was going to tell Russell about the extra money she'd received. Tianna walked out the room and back to the car with Russell. That's when he informed her that she had another date at the hotel down the street. Tianna smiled and nodded her head as Russell pulled out the parking lot.

CHAPTER TWO

Beep, Beep, Beep!

Beep, Beep, Beep!

Nakia's alarm chimed, waking her from a sound sleep. She rolled over before opening her eyes to confirm it was indeed five-thirty in the morning. She felt as though she'd just went to sleep five minutes ago, and now here it was, time to get up. Swinging the covers off her body, Nakia slid her feet into her fluffy pink house shoes and walked into her bathroom. Once she finished peeing, she brushed her teeth and walked to her children's rooms to wake them up for school. It was always harder to get her ten-year-old son, Rashaud, out of bed in the mornings, so she went into his room first.

"Rashaud, it's time to get up for school," Nakia called out, as she flipped the switch on the wall, giving the dark room light.

Rashaud didn't move. Instead, he laid there wrapped in his covers, snoring like a grown man that just worked an eight-hour shift. Shaking her head, she walked over to Rashaud's bed and pulled the covers off of him. When he still didn't move an inch, Nakia started shaking his shoulder lightly while calling his name.

"Huh?" He answered softly, as he opened his eyes just long enough to look up at his mother.

"It's time to get up for school."

"Aww, mom, five more minutes please?" Rashaud whined.

"Sorry Shaud, it's time to get up now."

Nakia exited the room and went down the hall to her seven-year-old daughter's room. She walked into the room, only to find Lexis sitting up in her bed watching television. Nakia walked over to her and sat next to her on her bed, wrapping her arm around her and pulling her in for a good morning hug.

"How long have you been up?" Nakia asked.

"Umm... I don't know. I watched two episodes of Peppa Pig; this is the third one," Lexis replied.

"Okay, well when this episode goes off, I want you to put on your clothes for school, then come down to the kitchen for breakfast."

"Okay mommy."

Nakia walked back into her room and took her shower. Once she was done, she brushed her shoulder length bark brown hair into a low ponytail. She then applied mascara to the already long eyelashes that graced her almond shaped eyes. Once she added lip gloss to her plump lips, her face was complete. Nakia never wore a lot of makeup and didn't need to. At thirty-two years old, her flawless skin didn't look a day over twenty-five.

When she was dressed in her gray and purple work uniform, Nakia went down to the kitchen to prepare a quick breakfast. She'd just got done scrambling the eggs when both her children walked into the kitchen. Nakia spooned the eggs onto three plates and added a piece of toast to each. Rashaud and Lexis took their plates and sat at the table. Nakia joined them and then sat down to a quick family breakfast.

"Don't forget that I have basketball tryouts after school today. They don't end until four-fifteen," Rashaud informed.

"Yes, I know. I don't get off until five today, so Uncle Jalyn is going to pick y'all up from school."

Jalyn was Nakia's younger brother who was more like her best friend. Anytime she needed him, she could count on him to be there. Ever since Rashaud and Lexis's father passed away three years ago, he had stepped up and played the role of their father. Being there for them with whatever they needed. Nakia was very thankful for Jalyn, knowing she wouldn't know what she would do without him.

Growing up, they knew from a young age that they were all they had. It was always them against the world. They'd been placed into the foster care system when Nakia was eight and Jalyn was six. After their mother tragically passed away in a horrible car accident on her way home from work, the two were never adopted and moved from foster home to foster home, until Nakia was eighteen. On the morning of her eighteenth birthday, she packed what little items Jalyn and she owned, and they left the foster home, never to look back.

Once breakfast was over, the family headed outside towards the car. The brisk Michigan spring air blew across Nakia's face, causing a cold chill to run through her body. She tightened her jacket around her, as she tried to shield her body from the cold. They all piled into Nakia's twelve-year-old Impala and pulled out her driveway. Pulling up to the school, Nakia kissed both of her children before they exited the car. Twenty minutes later and five minutes before the start of her shift, Nakia pulled into the parking lot of the Courtyard Marriot, where she'd worked for the past four years. She looked up at the five-story building and blew out a loud breath before getting out her car.

I swear I can't wait to get off. Nakia thought, as she walked into the hotel.

"Good morning," Bailey greeted with a smiled as Nakia walked into the office.

Bailey was forty-six and stood at five foot six inches tall with shoulder length brown hair, that had started to become gray at the roots. Her pail white skin was smooth, and she had small gray eyes that sat more so in the center of her face. Her fun and loving personality was what drew Nakia to her.

"Hey Bailey, how are you this morning?"

"I'm good, just a bit tired. I really didn't sleep well last night," Bailey replied.

"Hey Nakia, good morning," Anastasia greeted, as she walked into the office.

Anastasia was also in her late forties, standing at about five foot two. She had long blonde hair that she put different color streaks in every other week. This time they were purple. She had beautiful blue eyes that looked like the ocean of a private island, which went well with the purple in her hair.

Over the past four years, the three of them had become extremely close. They had formed a close bond, and Bailey even nicknamed them "the three amigos." Nakia couldn't stand her job; however with Bailey and Anastasia's goofy sense of humor, they always made the day go by faster. Bailey and Anastasia were both closer in age to each other, and about fifteen years older than Nakia, so to her, they were like older sisters. Her very white older sisters.

"Okay girls, I'm hungry. What are we going to get for lunch?" Bailey asked as she rubbed her stomach.

Anastasia and Nakia thought about it for a moment before they both yelled out Coney. There was a Coney Island right down the street from their job, and they ate there at least once a week. Nakia wrote down her order on an orange sticky note. A corned beef sandwich on an onion roll, with extra mayo, extra cheese, and extra pickles, and an order of chili cheese fries with a side of sour cream. She handed the sticky note and a twenty to Bailey.

"You know you always have the most difficult orders," Bailey said laughing.

"I just like what I like. And please make sure they don't forget the sour cream," Nakia laughed.

The work day went by rather quickly, and before Nakia knew it, it was time for her to clock out. She walked to her car and pulled out the parking lot. Nakia, not feeling up to cooking, stopped at Church's Chicken and grabbed dinner before heading home. When Nakia walked inside, Jalyn was sitting at the kitchen table helping Rashaud and Lexis with their homework. Nakia smiled at what a wonderful uncle Jalyn was to her children.

"Hey mama, guess what?" Rashaud beamed.

"I don't know, tell me?" Nakia replied, as she sat the Church's Chicken bag down on the kitchen counter.

"I made the team!" Rashaud yelled out, with the hugest smile on his face.

"That is wonderful, baby. I promise you, I'm going to be at every one of your games. I'm so proud of you, Rashaud."

"Thanks, mama. Are you gonna come to my games too, Uncle Jalyn?"

"I wouldn't miss them for the world, nephew," Jalyn replied.

"Lexis, how was your day at school?" Nakia asked.

"It was fine. We're learning our times tables, and my teacher says I'm doing really good. That's what my homework is tonight. I'm finished now. I didn't need Uncle Jalyn to help me at all. I did it all by myself, mommy."

"That's great, baby. Mommy is so proud of you. Are y'all hungry? I got some chicken."

"Yes!" They both yelled simultaneously.

"You staying for dinner, Jay?" Nakia asked.

"You already know."

Nakia laughed and began making the dinner plates. After dinner, Jalyn washed the dishes, and the kids went upstairs to take their showers. Once they were out and in their pajamas, Nakia tucked them into bed and went to take a shower herself. When she got out, she dried off and put lotion all over her body. She put on a white T-shirt and a pair of dark green boy shorts and got under her covers. She turned on Netflix before opening her nightstand drawer. Pulling out her ashtray, she lit the blunt that sat inside. This was always Nakia's time to herself. The kids were bathed, fed, in bed, and she was winding down from her day.

The next morning, Nakia's clock alarmed once again at five-thirty. It was Friday morning, so Nakia couldn't wait to get her day over with. It had been a long week, so she needed this weekend to relax and spend some quality time with her children. After getting the kids up, Nakia got dressed and went down to the kitchen to prepare breakfast. Nakia didn't care how tired she was or what time they woke up, her children would always have a hot breakfast before they went to school.

Once the kids had eaten and were dropped off at school, Nakia headed to work. She pulled into the crowded parking lot and shook her head, knowing it was about to be a busy day for her. She got out the car and walked into the hotel. Anastasia was standing at the computer, helping a guest with a reservation.

"Good morning, Anastasia. How are you today?" Nakia greeted.

"Good morning, I can't complain. It wouldn't do no good anyway," Anastasia replied.

"I feel you on that."

Nakia walked behind the front desk and went into the office to clock in. Bailey was sitting at her desk, assigning the rooms for the housekeepers to clean. She smiled and greeted Nakia when she saw her, and Nakia did the same. Nakia was just about to walk back up to the front desk when Anastasia rushed into the office.

"Girl, did you see that man I was checking in when you walked in?" Anastasia asked.

"Not really. Why, was he cute?"

"He's weird as hell. He was licking his lips and winking at me the entire time I was checking him in. And then, after I checked him in, he went out to the car and walked in with a female."

"Girl, you know that's how these dudes are," Nakia replied.

Nakia walked up to the front desk and began going through the list of arrivals for the day. She could tell by the eighty names on the arrivals list that today was going to be a busy day, and she couldn't wait until it was time for her to clock out. All she had to do was make it to five o'clock, and she wouldn't have to be back until Monday morning.

"Okay girls, I brought food today. It's in the break room. We got pasta salad, roast beef sliders, garden salad, and root beer floats. Now let's go eat," Bailey announced, as she took a few paper plates from the cubby and walked into the break room.

Knowing Nakia wasn't going to turn down any food, she followed Bailey with Anastasia close behind. They walked inside to see that Bailey had everything laid out on the counter. It looked like an all you could eat buffet.

"Damn, you got everything laid out all nice. What's the occasion, did I miss someone's birthday?" Anastasia asked.

"No, no. You know how I get into my cooking moods. Well, I couldn't sleep last night so I went down to my kitchen and this is what came out of that," Bailey replied.

The three of them piled food onto their plates, then walked back into the office to eat. They laughed and chatted over their delicious lunch. Nakia heard someone at the front desk yelling "hello" at what seemed like the top of their lungs. Rolling her eyes, Nakia got up from her seat and walked out to the desk to see what the costumer wanted.

"Hello, how can I help you?" Nakia asked. Copping a fake smile to make the guest think she really cared. In actuality, all Nakia wanted to do was get back to her plate of food.

"Hey, I wanted to know if there was a way that I could leave a key to my room at the front desk for someone?"

The man stood there, looking at Nakia and licking his lips. He winked at her, Nakia frowned up her face. I know this short ass nigga not standing here trying to flirt with me,. Nakia mused as she shook her head.

"Yes, you would just write their name down and when they get here, they have to present their ID to receive the key."

"But what if they don't have an ID?" The man asked.

"Well in that case, you wouldn't be able to leave a key for them. We have to check the ID before they receive a key. We can't just give a key to anyone walking off the street, sir."

"Okay, how about this? I can tell you what she looks like so when she comes in, you will know it's her," the man suggested.

At this point, Nakia was getting extremely irritated because she'd already told the guest the hotel's policy. No matter how many times he asked the same question in a different way, the answer would still be no. All Nakia wanted to do was get back to the food she had been rudely interrupted from moments ago.

"Sir, that will not work. If she doesn't have an ID, the only way she will get into the room is if you let her in," Nakia stated firmly.

The man nodded his head and walked away from the desk slowly, as if he was trying to think of something else to say. Nakia walked back into the office and sat down.

"Girl, that's the weird ass guy I was telling you about," Anastasia spoke.

Nakia laughed and nodded.

"Yeah, that dude is weird. He was up there trying to talk me into giving someone a key to his room without her having an ID," Nakia replied.

"Anastasia, didn't you say he walked in with a female?" Bailey asked.

"Yep, he sure did."

"And now he's wanting to leave a key for another woman? Y'all know what that means. He's fucking her right now and gonna let the other woman come while he takes her home," Bailey laughed.

"Yuck, I hope he gets them damn sheets changed," Nakia said.

The three women all laughed in unison and continued to have their lunch.

CHAPTER THREE

Russell sat on the edge of one of the two queen beds as he sent out several texts from the two phones he had in his hands. Occasionally, he looked up at Hannah to make sure she was making herself look right. Russell was never one to play about his money and never let anyone else play with it either. He ran a tight ship and made sure he kept it that way. Russell was a businessman, and he made sure he brought nothing but quality to his clients.

Hannah was a tall snow bunny with long blond hair and blue eyes. She didn't have much ass, but the thirty-four D breasts she had sitting up on her chest more than made up for it. She stood in the mirror applying her make up, and Russell sent out text after text. When she was done, she let him know she was ready. He looked her over from head to toe, making sure everything was in place, before he nodded his head in approval.

"Look lil baby, I'm gonna have to leave you at the spot with dude while I go pick the new girl up from the airport," Russell stated.

Hannah looked at Russell with wide eyes. He'd never made her go see a client alone before. She rolled her fingers around and shifted from one foot to the other. Hannah was scared. Not only to go see a client alone, but more so to tell Russell that she didn't want to do it. Her heart pounded as she parted her lips to speak.

"Russell, I've never been alone with a client before, and I don't think I should be. Muthafuckas is crazy out in the world, and I don't want to be alone with those crazy muthafuckas," Hannah said softly.

Russell didn't say a word. Instead, he continued sitting on the bed, looking down at his phones. At first, Hannah thought he wasn't paying her any attention and didn't hear her. So, she walked a bit closer to him and called his name. When he looked up at her, Hannah could see the rage in his eyes. Without her having any time to react, Russell jumped to his feet and grabbed her face, squeezing her cheeks tightly. His thumb on the right cheek and the other four fingers on the left, causing her lips to resemble a fish's lips.

"Bitch you don't get paid to think, you get paid to suck dick and bend over. I get paid to think, so you leave the fucking thinking to me. What you going to do and not going to do is strictly up to me. Now shut the fuck up and let's go!" Russell said firmly, as he pushed her head back so hard, it bounced off the wall.

With tears in her eyes, Hannah grabbed her purse and walked out the door with Russell right behind her. They took the stairs instead of the elevator and came out the back door and right to his truck. They both got in and Russell pulled off. A few moments later, he was pulling into the parking lot of a small raggedy motel. He pulled in front of room six, pulled one of his phones from his pocket, and shot a text to his client. A few moments later, the motel room door opened. Russell and Hannah stepped out of the SUV and walked into the room, one behind the other.

"You said you wanted the everything special, correct?" Russell asked, making sure he'd gave the guy the right price.

"Yes, that's right. I want everything," the man replied.

He was a middle aged, out of shape black man, with salt and pepper hair. He stood there in a pair of red basketball shorts and a white T-shirt. Hannah looked at him and tried to hide her true feelings. What does this old ass man want with me? Hannah asked herself. The man seemed to be old enough to be her father, and it made

Hannah even more uncomfortable. Just the thought of his old wrinkled up pecker anywhere near her body made her want to vomit.

"Okay, that's gonna be five hundred dollars," Russell stated.

The man pulled five hundred dollar bills out of his wallet and handed them to Russell. After counting them, Russell nodded his head and told Hannah that he would be back in an hour. Reluctantly, Hannah nodded her head okay and watched as Russell exited the room.

The man wasted no time, he pulled off his hoop shorts and sat on the bed. He had to spread his legs so that the tiny thing he called a dick could even be visible. Unconsciously, Hannah turned up her nose at the sight.

"Don't worry baby, he grows," the man said as he stroked himself while licking his lips.

Hannah forced a weak smile on her face because she knew it was no way possible it could grow that much. Saying that he had three inches was far too generous. I bet this man has to lean against the wall so he can reach the toilet to pee standing up. Hannah wanted to laugh out loud at the joke she'd just made to herself, however, she knew she couldn't. So instead, she sat her purse on the dresser and slowly walked over to the man. She pulled her red tube top down, exposing her large perky breasts. The man smiled and licked his lips, continuing to stroke himself as Hannah got completely naked.

"Come over here and show me what that mouth do," he moaned.

Hannah obliged and dropped to her knees in front of him. A musty smell entered her nose as soon as she positioned herself in front of his crotch. She wanted to jump to her feet and demand this overgrown man get in the shower and wash his smelly balls. However, she knew if she did that and he told Russell, it would be hell to pay. So instead, she placed her lips around his sweaty penis and began sucking. The man let out soft moans as though this was the best head he'd ever gotten. Hoping she could get him to cum fast, Hannah moved her tongue around the head of his dick. His moans grew louder, and he pushed the back of Hannah's head down, causing his small dick to go deeper into her mouth.

Hannah began to gag. Not because his manhood was beginning to choke her from the size because it definitely wasn't that. It was because the smell coming from the man was extremely potent. It had to be a sweat build up between the cresses of his thighs. This shit is just nasty, she thought. Her stomach was just about to force its contents out her mouth when the man pulled his dick from her lips.

"That shit was startin' to feel too good to me. I didn't want to bust a nut and not be able to get that tight pussy and ass that I've already paid for."

Hannah smiled, trying hard not to show the relief she truly felt. Standing up, Hannah got on the bed on all fours and arched her back. She heard the man as he unwrapped the condom, and she watched from the mirror on the walls as he put it on. He threw the gold condom wrapper and it landed next to Hannah on the bed. It took everything inside her not to bust out into laughter. The fact that this tiny dick muthafucka had the nerve to pull out a Magnum was comical. Three of that man's dicks could have been inside that one condom, and it would still be hella room left.

Grabbing both of Hannah's hips, the man plunged his dick inside her and instantly started moaning. Hannah couldn't feel a thing and didn't even know the man was inside her until she felt his stomach pounding against her ass.

"Aww, shit. This little pussy is so fucking tight. You gonna make me nut. Don't make me nut yet baby, I wanna get some of that ass too. Slow down baby, let me take my time in this pussy," he moaned.

That was all Hannah needed to hear, he had already paid, so if he came quickly, that would be his own problem. Hannah worked her hips and moved them three times in a circle. The man's moans grew louder and louder, and by the time Hannah was half way through the fourth circle, the man had came. He fell on top of Hannah, breathing heavily.

"Damn, that shit was good as hell," the man panted.

"Yes, it was baby," Hannah boasted, as she tried to scoot up from under the man.

Once she finally got to her feet, she took her belongings into the bathroom and began to freshen up. After she'd put her clothes back on and made sure her hair was in place, she looked at her phone to check the time. It was almost time for Russell to come back and pick her up.

She figured if she took her time in the bathroom, he would be there by the time she got out. So, she sat on the edge of the tub and began scrolling through Instagram. Five minutes later Russell was texting her, letting her know he was outside.

"When can I see you and that sweet pussy again?" The man asked, walking up to Hannah as soon as she exited the bathroom.

She smiled and let him know he would have to get with Russell and set up a date if he wanted to see her again. If there ever was a time in which he did, Hannah only hoped he showered first. She opened the motel room door and made her way out to Russell's SUV. She was just about to open the front passenger door when she noticed a light skinned girl sitting in the front seat. Russell rolled the window down halfway and told Hannah to get in the back seat. Hannah was already irritated by the fact she'd just fucked that stinky ass man, and now Russell was trying to put her in the back seat for some new bitch. This day was beginning to be too much for Hannah to handle. She wanted to go the fuck off, however, she thought twice about that, knowing it wouldn't end well for her. So, without a word, Hannah got into the backseat and Russell pulled out the parking lot.

"Hannah, this is Nicole but she goes by Nikki. Nikki, this is Hannah, she goes by Hannah," Russell joked.

"Hey," Nikki said.

"Hello," Hannah replied dryly.

"Are y'all hungry?" Russell asked.

"Yep!" both of the girls said.

Russell pulled into the parking lot of a Wendy's and pulled into the drive thru. Russell let both of the girls place their orders before he placed his. Once they'd gotten their food, Russell drove them back to the hotel. The party of three walked into the back door of the hotel and walked up the three flights of stairs to their room.

Hannah kicked her shoes off as soon as she entered the room. Plopping down on the bed and grabbing the Wendy's bag from Russell's hand. She pulled his burger and fries out the bag and handed them to him. She then took her food out the bag before dangling the bag in Nikki's direction. Nikki grabbed the bag before sitting on the other bed and removing the contents.

"Nikki, since you just got here, you won't be starting until tomorrow. We normally don't take off days, unless something really important comes up, but I'll make an exception for you," Russell said before turning to look at Hannah.

"You have an appointment in forty-five minutes, and you need to hurry up and eat so we can get ready to go," he continued.

Hannah nodded her head and began to eat her food. She watched Nikki as she ate and a small hint of jealousy entered her heart. She could look in her face and tell this girl was younger than her. Hannah wondered if she knew exactly what she had gotten herself into, or was she tricked by Russell the same way she was? When Hannah met Russell, he told her she would be dancing at private parties. At the third party, she was shocked when Russell told her how she had to suck this random man's dick in the bathroom for a hundred dollars. It was all downhill after that, at seventeen, Hannah had lost count of the men she'd given her body to.

Once they were done eating, Russell and Hannah left the room, leaving Nikki there alone. Seeing how she hadn't showered after getting off the plane, she went to her suitcase and pulled out a change of clothes. That one small suitcase housed everything that Nikki owned. She walked into the bathroom, turned on the hot water, and got in the shower.

Nikki met Russell on Instagram just a month prior. When he first hopped in her DM, it took her about two weeks to even respond. At first, she was scared because she didn't know him. She'd heard a lot of stories about people meeting online and then some crazy shit happened. Nikki definitely didn't want to end up on the news, so she stayed clear. Then one day, after coming home from school just to find out that her mother had sold all of the family's food stamps to feed her crack addition, she knew she could no longer take it anymore.

For as long as Nikki could remember, her mother had been on crack and always neglecting her children. They never had food, and when they did, it was only hot dogs or noodles. There were times Nikki had to wash up in the school bathroom because their water was turned off. The three-bedroom project apartment had one small couch in the living room. A card table with three folding chairs, and that's it.

Nikki and her brother Tony both slept on pallets in their rooms and their mother slept on the couch.

Once Nikki began talking to Russell, she found that he owned his own business. He'd told her she could come up to Detroit from Atlanta and could work for him. Russell had promised her a thousand dollars a week and a plane ticket to Detroit. To her young mind, the proposition sounded wonderful, almost too good to be true. She hated being at her mother's house. No one had cared about her, her entire life. Now here this man was ready to take her out of this hell and provide her with a wonderful life. She never even asked what the job was or anything. Russell bought the ticket, and Nikki got on the plane.

CHAPTER FOUR

Nakia slept in until nine thirty on Saturday morning, feeling extremely well rested when she woke up. She opened all the curtains in her room, and let the sun shine in. Nakia planned on spending the entire day with her children. For the past few weeks, she'd been too busy to have any family fun time. So today, she was gonna make up for lost time. She heard her children laughing and instantly knew they were in the kitchen. Smiling, Nakia walked out of her room and headed downstairs.

"What are you two laughing so hard about?"

"Rashaud was just showing me this really funny Tik Tok," Lexis beamed.

"Yeah ma, it's really funny. You want to see?" Rashaud asked.

"Yeah, play it," Nakia said, walking over to the table.

Rashaud pressed play on his iPad and Nakia watched as a man and a young boy danced to a song. The young boy was doing the dance well and seemed to know all the moves. The older man who Nakia assumed to be his dad was all over the place, not knowing how to dance at all. As soon as the man turned to the left, he tripped over his own feet and went tumbling down the stairs. Nakia joined in with the kids in laughter, as she shook her head.

"Y'all are not right for laughing at him," Nakia said, still laughing at the video.

"Aww ma, come on... you're laughing too," Rashaud said.

"Guess what we're having today?" Nakia cheered.

"What?" They both asked in unison.

"We're having family fun day. So, I need the two of you to go upstairs and get dressed," Nakia announced.

"Yayyyyy!" The children cheered, as they both ran upstairs to their rooms.

Nakia washed the bowls the kids used for their cereal, then headed to her room to get dressed for the day. Once everyone was dressed and ready to go, they got into Nakia's car and pulled out the driveway. Nakia had so much fun with her children, they went to the movies and to the arcade. By eight- thirty that night, they were all tired and ready to go home. Nakia couldn't help but laugh because she knew for Rashaud to want to leave all those games at the arcade, he must have been extremely sleepy.

Once they got home, everyone went to their bathrooms to shower. While the kids were in the shower, Nakia went into her bathroom and lit a blunt. They were all going to watch a movie in her room tonight; since Nakia didn't want her room to smell like weed, she smoked in the bathroom.

By the time Nakia was out the shower both Rashaud and Lexis were in her bed under the covers. She chuckled at them before walking up to the bed and sliding under the covers.

"We already picked the movie out mama; we were just waiting on you." Lexis said smiling, as she pressed play on the remote.

Nikki sat on the edge of the bed, as she listened to Russell explain to her how she would be working for him and the things she would have to do. She looked up at him with wide frightened eyes as he explained everything to her in detail.

"But Russell, I'm only fifteen. Don't you think these men will be upset when they come for sex with a grown woman and end up with me?" Nikki said, hoping her age would cause him to change his mind.

She had no clue this was what the job was. If she knew this was what he wanted her to do, she would have stayed in Atlanta. Nikki's heart beat fast as fear of what would happen next set in. She wanted to tell Russell no, but then what would happen? She was there in a different state with no money. He was the only person she knew in Detroit. If he told her to get out, Nikki would have nowhere to go, so she had to play this smart.

"That shit don't matter, these muthafuckas don't care about age. They paying for pussy, and you have one. Look Nikki, you told me you was ready to get to the money. You know that G a week we was talkin' bout? Well, this is how you get it," Russell said.

Nikki noticed the no nonsense tone Russell had taken and that scared her even more. She looked over to Hannah to see if she had anything to say about the situation. However, Hannah was standing in the corner smiling.

"How many men will I have to sleep with?" Nikki asked, clearly seeing there was no way around it.

"Anywhere from ten to twelve people," Russell answered.

"Ten to twelve men a week?" Nikki gasped.

Nikki was a virgin and had never given herself to anyone before. Now here Russell was telling her she would have a body count of a dozen in just a week's time. Just when she thought the grass was going to be greener on the other side, this shit happened.

"A week? Bitch you think you gonna make a thousand dollars a week from fucking twelve dudes a week? Dummy, that's how many you gotta fuck in a day. Fucking them in a week ain't gonna get you no money. Stupid ass lil girl. Russell, where the fuck did you get this bitch from?" Hannah chuckled.

"Hannah, watch yo fuckin' mouth. Did I ask you to say anything? I'm talking to her, now you shut the fuck up and go get ready. You have a john picking you up in twenty minutes."

"Pickin' me up? Russell, come on now, you have never let a john come pick me up, you have always come with me, and now I'm supposed to just go by myself? Yesterday, you dropped me off, didn't even stay with me. That was scary, but I did it. But this right here, nah. Russell, come on, you and I both know that shit not safe," Hannah pleaded with Russell to see things her way.

Russell looked into Hannah's eyes and saw she was truly frightened. Hannah had been down with him for years. So down in fact that if Russell was to choose a bottom bitch, it would be Hannah. So, instead of forcing her to do as he said, he nodded his head and said he would go down to the front desk and get another room for the night. Hannah nodded her head in agreement and continued to get dressed.

Russell made his way to the front desk and stood there waiting for the clerk to appear. He watched as a short blonde haired white woman, who looked to be in her early fifties, walk up to the desk.

"Hello, how can I help you?" She asked in a pleasant voice.

"Hi, Shelby," Russell said, looking down at her nametag.

"I'm already a guest here, I'm in room 323. I was wondering if the room next to me was available as well. Or at least one close to it?" Russell asked.

Shelby began looking through the computer, trying to help the guest. The room next to his was occupied, but the one across the hall was available. Russell let Shelby know that he wanted to rent the room for the next three days. Shelby gave Russell his total, and he inserted his visa card into the card reader. She handed him a key to room 325 and he walked back upstairs.

As soon as Russell walked off the elevator, his phone rang. When he looked at it, he saw it was Hannah's john calling. Russell hadn't gotten a chance to tell him that it had been a change of plans, so he was happy he'd called.

"What up, doe?" Russell said as he swiped the talk button.

"Hey, um Russell. I was just letting you know I was on my way to pick up a girl," the man's raspy voice spoke into the phone.

"Yeah, about that, there's been a change in plans. Instead of you picking her up, y'all gonna handle y'all business here. I just rented a room for y'all to get down in," Russell stated.

The john agreed and let Russell know he would be there shortly. When Russell got to the room, he handed Hannah the key to the other room and she walked out, headed to go meet her john.

"You feeling alright Nikki?" Russell asked.

She was sitting on the end of the bed, biting her bottom lip as she starred down at the floor. He walked up to her, placed his hand under her chin, and gently lifted her head, causing her to look him in the eyes. He could see the tears as they formed in her eyes.

"Russell, I'm scared. I had no clue I would have to do any of this. I'm only fifteen, and I'm a virgin," Nikki whispered, as she tried to wipe the tears that fell.

Russell looked at her with wide eyes. A virgin? Russell never would have thought. Now a days, he knew fifteen-year-olds with one or two children. The fact she was a virgin was rare. Russell smiled as dollar signs flashed through his mind. Knowing he'd just stumbled upon a goldmine, he knew he would have to handle Nikki very carefully.

Russell walked over to Nikki and sat beside her, wrapping his arms around her and pulling her in tightly. He wanted her to feel safe with him. Russell knew that if he could get into her head, he could get into everything else. He was a pro in the game of manipulation, and it was time to work his magic.

"Why didn't you tell me you were a virgin?" Russell whispered.

"I didn't know I had to. When you asked me to come up here, you never said I would be coming up here to be a damn prostitute."

"Nah, we don't use that word around here. I don't fuck with no prostitutes. Prostitutes are cheap and don't make the money we make. I run a successful business giving my clients the ultimate fantasy. You girls are just ambassadors for my company. Fantasy experts if you will."

Nikki looked over at Russell and smiled before chuckling a little. Russell smiled back, knowing she was starting to loosen up a bit. Russell could get what he wanted from any woman walking this earth, so he knew in a short time, Nikki would be bringing in the money just like the rest of his bitches. He would just have to play this role for a moment until Nikki started to trust him.

"Listen, I don't want you to feel uncomfortable here, so we can take things slow at first. If you don't want to stay, then you can leave whenever you want. You said you wanted to come here, so I brought you here. If you want to leave you can walk right out that door.

However, if you do want to stay, you're going to have to put in work just like everybody else."

Even if Nikki wanted to go back to Atlanta with her crackhead mother in their empty project apartment, how would she get back? She had no money to get on a plane or a bus. So, at least for now, she would have to stay with Russell. She could work for him and save her money. If she didn't like being there, she could take her money and come up with a plan to leave. So, after weighing her options, she agreed to work for Russell.

"Cool, I was hopin' you would say that, because I didn't want you to leave," Russell smiled at Nikki, making sure to show all thirty-two of his pearly white teeth.

Russell ran his hand over Nikki's cheek. He felt her body tense up and then placed his other hand on her thigh. He knew if she was nervous around him, she would be ten times that around the clients, and he couldn't have that. He knew he needed to break her in, and with Hannah being out the room, now was the perfect time.

"Don't be nervous, daddy got you," Russell whispered, as he ran his hand across her perky breasts. "I'm 'bout to show you how to please a man," Russell asserted.

Nikki's heart began to beat rapidly in her chest as her nerves set in. She knew Russell was about to break her virginity and it frightened her because she didn't know what to expect. Nikki never thought it would happen like this. She pictured giving her body away to the man she loved, in a room full of scented candles and soft music. Instead, she was about to pop her cherry for the man she hardly knew. Nikki knew if she wanted to stay in Detroit and work for him, she would have to do what he wanted. She remained still as Russell rubbed on her small breasts, pulling one from her shirt and popping her nipple into his mouth.

"Take off your clothes," Russell stated.

Nikki stood to her feet and did as she was asked. She stood there in front of Russell as he admired her naked body. Placing her hands over her chest, she tried to cover herself. The way Russell was staring at her like she was a steak dinner made her feel uncomfortable. Russell felt Nikki tense up even more when he palmed her bare breast.

"You need to calm down. You can't be acting like this when you around clients, relax baby," Russell encouraged.

Nikki watched as Russell walked over to the nightstand. He gabbed something out of the top drawer before walking back over to her.

"Here, take this. It will help you relax," Russell stated, handing Nikki a small pink pill.

"What is it?" She asked, taking the pill from Russell.

"It's molly, it will make you feel good," Russell informed.

Nikki had watched what drugs had done to her mother and couldn't see herself being that way. She also knew she was going to have to work, and if this little pill would make her comfortable while doing so, then she would take it. Fuck it, it's just one little pill, just to take the edge off. What's the worst that could happen? Nikki placed the pill on her tongue and swallowed it then watched Russell do the same.

"It's gonna take about a half hour for it to kick in. In the meantime, though, just relax. Once the molly takes over, you gonna be good," Russell stated.

Nikki laid back on the bed as she waited on the drug to take its effect. Before she knew it, Russell had her pants down and had his face between her thighs. She moaned softly as his warm wet tongue tickled her love button. Normally, Russell would have never gone down on one of his hoes. However, Nikki had fresh, never been touched pussy, so Russell couldn't help but taste it. His dick hardened as he listened to Nikki moan in pleasure.

Russell could tell the molly was starting to kick in when Nikki started pinching her own nipples and moaning louder. He pulled his tongue from her hole and watched as her flowing juices puddled underneath her.

"Can daddy feel this pussy, baby?" Russell breathed.

Without protest, Nikki grabbed Russell's erect manhood and guided him inside her. Clenching up as his largeness broke the space between girl and woman, her tightness caused Russell to bite down on his bottom lip as he tried not to scream out like a bitch. They were right in the middle of mind-blowing sex when Russell's phone began ringing. Not wanting to stop, he kept pumping in and out of Nikki until his phone rang again. Knowing it was money on the line, Russell rolled off Nikki and answered it.

"What up, doe?" Russell answered. "What? You gonna have to calm down... I can't understand you when you doing all that crying."

"What?!" Russell yelled, as he jumped up from the bed.

Nikki was so high, it took her several seconds to notice that Russell was no longer on top of her, let alone in the bed. He was standing in the corner, rushing to put on his clothes.

"Is everything okay?" Nikki asked.

"No, one of my hoes just got robbed for all her day's profits. This is some bullshit!" Russell yelled.

"I gotta go get her, and when I find the muthafucka that robbed her, I'm gonna fuck his ass up!" Russell continued.

Once he slid into his white Force Ones he opened the top drawer of the nightstand and pulled out a chrome pistol that he tucked in his waistline before exiting the room. Russell ran down the stairs in lighting speed as he made his way to his SUV. Anger shot through his body as he thought about what he was going to do to the muthafuckas that were playing with his money.

Russell pulled into the parking lot of the motel and saw Tianna sitting on the curb crying. He put his car in park and jumped out, rushing over to Tianna. His rage was damn near seeping from his pores, and he was ready for any smoke that came his way.

"Where them niggas at? What the fuck happened?" Russell roared frantically, as he pulled Tianna to her feet.

"I don't know. I was in the room with one of my johns, servicing him the way he asked. I dropped to my knees to suck his dick, and the next thing I know, I was being hit in the head with something. When I woke up, he was gone and so was all the money. Everything happened so fast, that I didn't have any time to react. As soon as I woke up, the first thing I did was call you," Tianna cried, clearly scared of Russell's reaction.

"How much money was it?"

"A little over five racks," Tianna stated.

"Fuuuucck!" Russell yelled.

Five thousand dollars was a lot to lose in one day, and Russell didn't understand how something like this could even happen. Tianna knew she was never supposed to have that much money on her at one time, that had been one of the rules ever since she started doing jobs on her own. Tianna worked alone because Russell thought that she could handle herself. Russell made sure she stayed strapped with a pistol, a teaser, and a small can of mace everywhere she went. Russell also made sure Tianna knew that after every other john, she was supposed to take her money home and keep it there until Russell came and got it that night. She knew she was never to be out with more than five hundred dollars on her at once, so Russell couldn't understand why she had broken his rules. His blood boiled, as he clenched his fist tightly, trying to resist the urge to punch Tianna directly in her mouth for disobeying him.

"Who the fuck was the john? I didn't send him to you, so where the fuck did he come from?"

That was yet another rule of Russell's that had been broken. None of his girls were ever to go with a john that he didn't send to them, out of fear of it being the police. Tianna knew that better than anyone, and Russell's patience was wearing thin with each passing minute.

"I-I met him while I was waitin' on my Uber after my last john. He came up to me and told me he would pay me five hundred for me to give him a prostate massage while I sucked him off. I couldn't pass it up Russell. Five hundred, and I didn't even have to give up no pussy? That shit was easy money. He even gave me the money up front so I didn't think he was on no bullshit, but then the fuck boy robbed me," Tianna cried.

Russell clenched his jaws as he listened to Tianna tell her side of the story. He couldn't believe he'd just been robbed. Out of all the time he'd been pimping hoes, he'd never once been robbed and knew it was due to the strict rules he'd set in place. Now, in one night, one hoe had broken two of those rules, which left her to be robbed for her entire day's earnings.

"Get in the truck, we bout to go find this nigga! Do you remember what he looked like?"

"Not really, Russell. I see a lot of dudes everyday. All I know is he was skinny with dreads. Other than that, I don't remember anything," Tianna spoke.

Pissed, Russell pulled out the parking lot of the motel and headed back to Tianna's house. He wasn't going to take this loss; this was her fault for not following the strict rules he'd set. Tianna was now in debt, and she had no choice but to work off every penny, no matter how long it took.

"Go get changed and freshen up, and don't take all day. I'll be sittin' right here waitin' on yo ass," Russell declared.

"Waitin' on me for what?" Tianna asked, looking at Russell confused as she waited on him to answer.

"Bitch so you can work off the money you lost, fuck you thought?"

"Russell please, my head is hurtin' from being hit in it. I'm tired from workin' all damn day, and I just want to go inside, take a hot shower, and get some sleep."

"And I just want my fucking money, the money that you lost, bitch. The faster I get what I want, the faster you get what you want. Now got get yoself together and don't keep me fuckin' waiting," Russell stated firmly.

Reluctantly, Tianna slowly got out of the SUV and walked inside her house. She knew Russell would be mad about her being robbed, but she had no clue he would make her work off the money in the same night. It was almost eleven at night, and Tianna was more than exhausted. She walked into the bathroom and turned on the hot water, showering as quickly as possible. Knowing Russell was already mad, she didn't want to add to his frustration. Within twenty minutes she was dressed and walked back out the door.

"I got three jobs lined up for you already, and because you can't hold yo own and not get robbed, I gotta sit at all of them with you. I swear if you let this shit happen ever again, I'm gonna fuck you up. You understand me?" Russell asserted firmly, as he wrapped his hand around Tianna's neck.

Tianna nodded her head in understanding, hoping Russell would take his hand off her neck. Russell had never put hands on her before, and when she looked into his eyes, it was like the devil was looking back at her. It was at that moment she decided if she did steal from

Russell again, she would come up with a more strategic plan. She was sick of selling her pussy and giving all the money to Russell. When he came to her with the plan, the amount of money he offered her sounded good. However, when Tianna turned in thousands of dollars to him every night, she began to think smarter.

She now understood not just the power of the pussy, but she understood the power of her own pussy. She knew that if she was able to build her own cliental, she would be able to work for herself and keep all her profits. However, everyone in Detroit went through Russell if they were paying for pussy. Going against Russell in the business could deem fatal for Tianna, and she wasn't ready to risk her life. Russell let Tianna's neck go but kept his eyes on her for several seconds before pulling off and heading to the motel.

"I'll collect the money, your hands can't touch no more til' I see fit," Russell said.

He turned up his nose and looked over at Tianna like she was the juice in the bottom of a trash bag. In his eyes, that's exactly what she was, garbage juice. A bitch playing with his money was equivalent to a bitch spiting in his food, and either way a bitch could get bodied. Russell liked Tianna and didn't want to make an example out of her, but he would if this shit ever happened again.

Both Russell and Tianna got out of the SUV and walked up to the motel room door. The john must have been watching from the window, because the door swung open before Russell even had a chance to knock.

"Hey, I thought y'all wasn't coming. You ten minutes late," the young man said.

Russell busted out laughing at the young guy's eagerness. He knew the guy was probably a virgin and this was going to be the first time he smelled pussy since he came out of his mama at birth. He was short and skinny, with brown hair and glasses. He resembled Fogell from the movie Superbad.

"What's funny?" The guy asked. Opening the door wider so Russell and Tianna could step inside the room.

"Yo man, how old are you?" Russell asked, still laughing.

"I'm eighteen. In fact, my birthday was just last week. Would you like to see my ID?" He replied.

Not even Tianna could hold her laughter in this time. Did this dude really just ask us if we wanted to see his ID? Where the fuck do Russell find these people at? Tianna thought to herself, laughing so hard that tears fell from her eyes.

"Nah dude, all that is not necessary, all I need from you is the money," Russell stated.

"Oh yeah, that's right. I'm sorry, this is my first time doing something like this," he replied, looking around the room for his wallet.

"Yeah, we can tell," Russell responded.

Once the john had located his wallet, he handed Russell five one-hundred-dollar bills. This was the most money he'd spent on any one thing in his eighteen years on earth but looking at Tianna's sexiness let him know this was an investment. Her thick thighs and perky breasts let him know the stock for pussy was up, and he was cashing in.

Russell let Tianna know he would be outside in the SUV and just to come out when she was done. Tianna nodded her head and sat her purse on the dresser, as she watched Russell walk out the door.

"What's yo name, baby?" Tianna asked, as she pulled the spaghetti straps of her purple satin mini dress down over her shoulders, exposing her breasts.

The john swallowed the lump in his throat before replying to her.

"My name is Larry," he replied nervously.

Yeah, this goofy nigga looks like a damn Larry. Tianna joked to herself, as she tried not to laugh.

"How bout I just call you daddy? I like that better. So, tell me, daddy, what is it that you want me to do to your body?" Tianna asked seductively.

Larry fell over on the bed in laughter, as he held his stomach. At this point it was Tianna that was confused, had she missed the joke?

"What's funny?" Tianna asked, raising her left eyebrow.

"You, that was hilarious. Look at me, we both know I'm nowhere near old enough to be your father, silly goose," Larry said, as he slapped his knee.

"Just take off your pants," Tianna admonished, rolling her eyes.

Russell didn't drop Tianna off until four that following morning, and she was running on fumes by that point. Her pussy was sore from being pounded on by so many dudes in such a short time span. All she wanted was for Russell to give up her cut of the profits so she could go soak in some hot water.

"Fuck you waiting on, get out the car, bitch. I'm tired and want to go to sleep. You holdin' me up just sittin' here like this," he stated coldly.

"You haven't given me my profits yet," Tianna replied.

Russell looked at Tianna for a moment, confused on if she was serious or not. Once he realized she was, he answered her.

"Bitch, yo cut of the work for today was stolen, or did you forget? Get the fuck outta my ride with this bullshit."

Tianna looked at Russell in shock. There was no way he was serious, she had put in extra work to make the money up for Russell. Granted, she had been the one to steal the money, however, Russell didn't know that, so Tianna felt him not giving her a cut was flat out wrong. There was no way Tianna was going to be played. She was the player in any game that came up.

"Oh, hell nah, Russell. I worked hard for that money, and I want my cut. You not just gonna keep my money, nigga," Tianna yelled, causing spittle to fly from her mouth.

She didn't know where she grew the balls from, but the words had already come from her mouth, so she couldn't back down now. She starred into Russell's eyes, not moving an inch, as she waited for him to count out her money. Russell removed his hand from the wheel, but instead of reaching into his packet, he backhand slapped Tianna right in the mouth.

"Ahh," Tianna screamed, as he placed her hand over her mouth and felt the wetness of the blood running from her busted lip.

"Bitch don't you ever fix yo lips to come at me outta pocket, fuck wrong with you? I see I done been too nice to yo high yellow ass. But fucked up is what you got me," Russell yelled, as he punched Tianna in the side of her head several more times.

"Hoe, get yo trash ass out my fuckin' truck before I really show you what's up," Russell continued to yell.

Scared and bleeding, Tianna grabbed her purse and rushed out of Russell's SUV. She ran to her door like he was directly behind her, chasing her. It wasn't until she closed and locked the door behind her that she was able to breath. Tianna went to sleep that night, knowing it was time for her to get the fuck away from Russell and to work for herself.

CHAPTER FIVE

Nikki laid in the bed as she waited on Russell to return, she was so high and feeling so good that all her fears had went away. She wanted him to come back and continue to touch her the way he had. Nikki turned over and looked at the clock, it was a quarter after four in the morning. Damn, where is he? I hope everything is okay. Nikki thought to herself, and as if Russell heard her, he walk through the door.

"You good, Russell?" Nikki asked, sitting straight up in bed.

"Yeah, I'm straight. One of my girls had some wild shit going on, and I had to handle it. Everything good now. I'm just a little tired."

"Too tired to finished what we started before you left?"

Russell looked Nikki up and down and knew she was still high off the molly from earlier. He wanted to be the first to try out what she had to offer, however, he was running off no energy. All he wanted was a shower and the bed.

"Daddy's tired now, baby, but when I get up, it's gonna be you and me," he replied.

Disappointed, Nikki nodded her head and laid back in the bed, as Russell went into the bathroom. She had no clue how she had gone from scared to comfortable in such a short time, but she knew the pill

Russell had given her had played a major part of it. She didn't want to keep taking them and get addicted. However, if they helped her to become comfortable with her job, she would take them as needed.

"Where is Hannah?" Russell asked, as he exited the bathroom.

"She stayed in the other room," Nikki told him.

Russell nodded his head, got into bed next to her, and pulled her close to him. He wasn't a cuddler, however, Russell was a master at manipulation, so he would do anything possible to make sure he secured the bag.

"Can I lay with you?

"Yeah," Nikki whispered.

The two of them fell asleep, and the next morning, Russell did just as intended and broke Nikki in. The look on her face when he was finished let him know he would be able to get Nikki to do anything he wanted her to do, and that's exactly how he wanted it to be.

"Go get in the shower and get dress. I'm about to go get Hannah so y'all can start work. It's money to be made, and we have to get to it."

Nikki got right up and went to the bathroom. This was it, and it wasn't any turning back now. It was time to get this money, and no matter if Nikki stayed with Russell or not, she was going to need it, so she had to do what she had to do. Once out the shower, Nikki dressed in a pair of tight jeans and a white tank top. She slicked her hair back into a low ponytail, making sure she brushed her edges to perfection. Once her hair was to her liking, she placed clear lip gloss on her lips and huge gold hoop earrings in her ears. Nikki smiled at herself as she looked in the mirror before walking out the bathroom.

"I'm ready," she announced.

Both Russell and Hannah just stood there looking at Nikki, like they had no clue what was going on.

"Ready for what?" Hannah asked for clarification.

"To go to work. What you mean? Are we not working today anymore?"

Hannah busted out laughing so hard, she almost fell over. Nikki stood there looking at Hannah confused. Why the fuck is this bitch laughing so hard? Fuck is funny? Nikki asked herself.

"Bitch ain't nobody gonna pay for you lookin' like that. You really think you look fuckable? This shit funny as hell, Russell, I know you fuckin' lyin', this cannot be yo new bitch. This hoe just a waste of space," Hannah stated, looking at Nikki in pure disgust.

Before Nikki could say a word, Russell stepped in. "Yo Hannah, shut the fuck up. Why the fuck you always talkin'? You need to learn to shut yo mouth sometimes. You been getting outta pocket way too much lately. I'm beatin' yo ass next time you do that shit, just know that."

With that, Hannah stopped laughing completely and was now standing there straight faced. She didn't know Russell would be this mad by her statement, because they both knew it was true. Their job was to sell the fantasy, and right now, Nikki didn't look like anybody's fantasy. However, the threat of an ass whippin' assured that Hannah wouldn't say anything else.

"Now Nikki," Russell continued. "When you are on the job, you have to be sexy. Show some skin, some titties, and a lil ass. You gotta show them niggas they gonna get they money's worth before they even pay for you. This look you got going don't say none of that, so Imma need you to change."

"But I don't have anything else. All I have is four pair of jeans and a few shirts. This was literally the best outfit I could put together. I don't know what you want me to do," Nikki admitted in defeat.

Russell nodded his head, put on his shoes, and told Nikki that he was taking her shopping. He couldn't fault her for being green to the game, he just knew he would have to teach her. Russell knew if Nikki could master the game, she would make him a lot of money, and that was all he wanted.

"Can I go too?" Hannah asked. "I need some new clothes."

"Nah bitch, stay here and think about why you shouldn't fuckin' speak when nobody speakin' to you," Russell stated harshly before walking out the door with Nikki right behind him.

Russell and Nikki spent hours shopping at Westland and Fairlane malls. By the time they were done, Russell had spent well over six hundred dollars and Nikki was all smiles. Never in her life had someone did anything like this for her, not even her mother. So, this alone made her think Russell really cared about her. Maybe being with him is the right decision, Nikki concluded, walking through the mall with her head held high.

"You hungry?" Russell asked, looking over at Nikki.

"Yeah, I could definitely eat," she replied.

The two made their way to the food court and picked their desired restaurants before sitting at the table and eating. Halfway through the meal Russell's phone rang. Looking down at it, he saw it was Tianna.

"What up doe?"

"Hey Russell, I know you probably still mad at me. I just wanted to know if I was working by myself today or if you was coming to get me?" Tianna asked.

Russell rolled his eyes before taking a bite of his chicken shawarma. He knew he couldn't let Tianna work alone today with her just getting robbed. However, he wanted to focus on Nikki today with it being her first day on the job. It was time for him to have all his bitches together, so he could watch them all.

"Yeah, I'm comin' to get you. Pack you up a few things cuz you gonna be with me for a few days. You fucked up bad last night, so that showed me we need to really get to the money. You let a nigga catch you slippin' so obviously I ain't been teachin' you enough. I'll be there in about an hour, so be ready," Russell stated.

"Okay, I'll be ready," Tianna said before ending the call.

Once Russell and Nikki were done eating, they gathered all her bags and headed to Russell's SUV. Just like she was told, Tianna was ready when Russell pulled up. She placed her red Adidas duffle bag in the trunk before getting into the backseat.

"Tianna, this is Nikki. Nikki, this is Tianna," Russell introduced.

"Hey," They both said in unison.

Russell knew he would at least have to get one more room now that he'd brought over another girl. In order for him to be able to work all three at the same time, he would need three rooms. So, when he got to the hotel he sent the girls upstairs and went to the front desk.

"Hello, how can I help you?" Shelby asked cheerfully.

"Hi, I need another room for three days, and I need it to be close to 323 and 325. I have some family comin' in," Russell stated.

Shelby punched a few keys on the keyboard and searched the

computer before speaking. "The closest I can get you is room 331. The total after tax for the three nights is four hundred-thirty-seven dollars and twenty-three cents."

"Cool," Russell said before inserting his debit card into the card reader. Shelby handed Russell the keys to his room and he walked away. He could smell the money in the air as all three girls dressed themselves in sexy lingerie. He logged onto the apps in his phone and let everyone know he was now open for business.

Tianna stood in front of the bathroom mirror of her room mad as hell. She was on her third john and hadn't been able to put up no money for herself. Russell was watching her like a hawk and collecting every dollar himself. She was never gonna be able to get any money this way. Tianna had been taking a cut off top for weeks now and Russell hadn't noticed. She had fucked up by lying about a robbery, now she couldn't get his eyes off her. Tianna's phone buzzed, she looked down and opened the text from Russell, letting her know her next john would be there in ten minutes.

"Girl, it's something going on in those rooms. Those girls are prostitutes or something. I seen a bunch of different men going in and out of each of the rooms yesterday. Soon as one leaves, another one coming right behind him. They look young as hell, and the guy who's with them is probably trafficking those girls," Bailey declared as soon as Nakia walked into the back office on Monday morning.

"What rooms, what girls, and what guy?" Nakia inquired, ready to sip on the hot tea that was being poured.

"That weird guy on the third floor with them two girls. Bailey is convinced that something is going on in that room, and it's another young girl with them now," Anastasia replied.

"What? Like he they pimp or some shit?" Nakia inquired.

"Yes, he is sex trafficking those young girls, I know he is," Bailey stated.

"That is fucking horrible, you can look in their faces and tell they're young," Anastasia said.

"Damn, that is fucked up. I couldn't image my daughter being out here like that," Nakia spoke.

After the brief conversation, Nakia walked up to the front desk and began her work. About two hours into her workday, she noticed one of the girls from the room walk down to the lobby. She stood at the door like she was waiting on someone. Nakia tried not to make it obvious that she was looking at the girl, but she couldn't help it. The girl was dressed in a black and white snake skinned two-piece bra and short set, with thigh high black boots. Her shoulder length hair was brushed up into a ponytail at the top of her head that feathered out and a black ribbon tied around it. She had on enough make-up to beat Nakia's, Bailey's, and Anastasia's faces to the gods. She thought the make-up would make her look older, however, it was the hairstyle that let Nakia know.

"Damn, she can't be no more than fourteen or fifteen years old," Nakia whispered to herself.

As a mother herself and a former child of the system, Nakia could only image what that child must have been through to feel like this was her only choice for survival at such a young age. Her heart sank when a car pulled up and the young girl walked out to the car and walked inside with a man just a few moments later. The man looked old enough to be her father, but the way he was touching on her body let Nakia know he wasn't. It was at that moment Nakia knew then that what Bailey was saying was true.

"We gotta do something about this," Bailey whispered, as she walked up to Nakia.

"Shit, you scared the shit outta me. I didn't even see you coming." Nakia jumped.

"That's because you were too busy watching that young girl. I told you they were being trafficked. We gotta do something about this, and fast," Bailey stated.

Nakia looked at Bailey confused as to what she meant. "Girl, what do you think we can do?" Nakia asked.

"We need to call the police; we can't just sit here and watch this happen. Those girls are someone's daughters. If this was your daughter, wouldn't you want someone to help her?"

Nakia thought for a moment. She didn't want to get involved in anyone else's drama, especially when it involved the police. Growing up the way Nakia did, the police were never the ones you call when trouble came. If you saw the police, they were the trouble. However, what Bailey said was correct. She would want someone to help her daughter in a situation like this.

"Whatever you want to do Bailey," Nakia said reluctantly.

"If they still here tomorrow, then I'm calling.

CHAPTER SIX

Russell laid in his bed and thought about all the money he'd made in just one day. He counted ten thousand dollars for himself, and that was after he'd given the girls their cut. Having them close to him, all working out of the same hotel was a genius idea, and he had no clue why he didn't think of it sooner. The only bad thing about it was that he always had to sit in his SUV when all the rooms were in use. He wanted to get a fourth room, but the rooms were running him damn near two-hundred dollars apiece each night. With that, Russell decided they would move to a cheaper hotel the next day.

Getting out of bed, he went to each girl and told them to pack their shit up so they would be ready to go in the morning. With this being their last night there, Russell decided they should make the night special.

"When y'all get done packing, take showers and meet me in my room," he stated.

All the girls nodded their heads and went on to do as they were told. An hour later they were all in Russell's room sipping on Casamigos and each had to pop a molly. Russell knew how to get them in freak mode, and that's exactly what that combination would do.

"Y'all get naked," Russell instructed.

All three girls stood to their feet and began taking off what little they had on. Russell instructed each girl on what to do to the next. Placing his hand in his pants, he stroked himself as he watched. When he was done watching and wanted to get down on the action, he had the girls join him in bed, and they began pleasing him well into the night.

The next morning, Russell woke up bright and early. He dropped Tianna off at home and told her to pack a few items for the next few days. He could tell by the look on Tianna's face that she didn't agree with going back to another room, but he didn't care. She was the one that fucked up, and in return, Russell had come up with a master plan.

"Don't keep me waiting either, I'll be back in a few hours."

"But Russell, why can't I just work the way I...."

Before Tianna could even finish her sentence, Russell punched her in the mouth, breaking the skin on her lip for a second time in the matter of days. If working for Russell meant that she would have to be abused, then she would pass. She didn't need him; she could go in business for herself and keep all the money she made.

"Look Russell, I'm getting sick of you putting your damn hands on me. This was not what I signed up for!" Tianna yelled.

"Bitch let me tell you something, when you signed up to work for me, you signed up for everything that comes with it. When any one of my hoes get out of pocket, I'm puttin' them back in that shit. You ain't no different bitch," Russell snapped back.

"Well, what if I don't want to be one of your bitches anymore? What if I'm sick of this bullshit? Not only do I sell my pussy and you keep more than half the money, but now you got the nerve to be puttin' hands on me? Oh, hell nah, I ain't with this shit, Russell."

Without a word, Russell pulled his pistol from his waist and hit Tianna in the head with the butt of it so hard, she swore she saw stars. Her head bounced off the window and she had to place both hands on her forehead to stop it from spinning. Tears welled up in her eyes, as she tried to process the fact that Russell had just hit her with his gun.

"W-why would you hit me like that?" Tianna cried, as blood trickled down her forehead.

Russell didn't speak. Instead, he got out his truck, walked around to the passenger side, and swung the door open. With one hand he pulled Tianna out the car and practically drug her to her front door.

"Russell, please stop," Tianna pleaded, as she fought as hard as she could to break away from his grasp.

"Bitch, shut the fuck up before you have yo neighbors in my fuckin' business. Now open the fuckin' door."

Tianna pulled her keys from her purse. However, she was shaking so badly, that she dropped them on the ground before she could put the correct key in the lock. Russell kicked her in the stomach when she bent down to pick them up, and Tianna screamed as she fell over.

"Bitch, get yo dramatic ass up and open this fuckin' door before this ass whippin' gets worse," Russell threatened.

Once inside the house, Russell threw blow after blow which landed on Tianna's body and face, as she screamed out in agony and pleaded with Russell to stop, but it all fell on deaf ears.

"You think you can just leave me?" Punch. "Yo ass can't leave until I say you can." Kick. "This shit ain't over til' I say it's over." Slap.

Tianna screamed as each hit landed, sending excruciating pain throughout her entire body. She prayed to God for him to send his angels to protect her life and begged him not to allow Russell to kill her. She balled up into a fetal position until Russell became tired and stopped hitting her. Out of breath, Russell took a seat on Tianna's couch and lit a cigarette. He inhaled deeply before he spoke.

"Look what the fuck you made me do. Now we both gonna miss out on money all because you can't keep yo mouth shut. Look at me when I'm talkin' to you!"

Tianna, still laying in the same position on the floor, knew she needed to do exactly what he said so things wouldn't get any worse. She gathered all her strength and turned to face Russell, groaning from the pain with each movement. Tears ran down her eyes as she looked into Russell's eyes.

"You mine, bitch, until I say otherwise. I might let you go, I might not. Either way that's up to me to decide. You understand me?"

"Yes, Russell," Tianna answered weakly.

"Tell me... tell me you mine."

"I'm yours," she replied weakly.

"Til' when?" Russell tacked on.

"Til' you say otherwise."

Nakia walked into her house only to find Jalyn and Rashaud sitting in her living room playing the latest version of 2K. A half-eaten pizza sat on the coffee table right in front of them with the box opened. Several empty Pepsi and Mountain Dew cans lay scattered across the living room floor. After the day she had, all she wanted to do was take a long hot bath and sip on a glass of wine. Coming home to her living room being a mess was not part of the plan.

"Come on y'all, why y'all got my house lookin' like this? If this is what y'all was gonna do, the least y'all could have did was clean it up before I got home," Nakia fussed.

"My bad, sis, I lost track of time playin' this game with Shaud. Lil nigga beat me, and I needed my rematch. I got you though, it's bout to look like this shit never happened in like twenty minutes. Let us just finish this last quarter. They ate though, so at least you don't have to cook," Jalyn stated.

Nakia nodded her head. "Thank you. Where is Lexis?"

"Upstairs in her room watching cartoons. She got tired of watchin' us play the game," Rashaud answered.

"I'm gonna go take a bath, please have my living room clean by the time I come back," Nakia said.

"We got you, sis, you know that. Gone take yo lil bubbly with them candles and shit. Relax, Uncle Jay got this shit."

"If you had it, the living room wouldn't be looking like this," Nakia laughed before walking upstairs.

Opening Lexis' room door, she found her sitting on her bed watching her favorite cartoon, Peppa Pig. Nakia stood there for a moment and smiled at her baby girl.

"Hey baby, how was your day?"

"Hey mommy! I missed you so much," Lexis said, jumping off her bed and running up to Nakia.

"I missed you too, Lexi," Nakia beamed, as she bent down to hug her daughter.

"You wanna watch Peppa Pig with me?"

"Sure do, right after I take a bath. We can have a pajama party," Nakia answered.

Lexis smiled and nodded her head yes, letting Nakia know she was extremely excited. Nakia told Lexis she would be back soon, and she went to run her bath. She poured herself a half a glass of wine. A whole glass would get her tipsy, and she didn't want to be drunk while she watched cartoons with her daughter. She sipped her wine, as she laid out her two-piece pink and white flannel pajamas. She sat down in the tub full of bubbles and tried to relax her day away. However, the images of those young girls played over and over in her head.

Once out the tub, Nakia applied lotion to her body and put on her pajamas before heading back into Lexis' room. She opened the door, only to find Lexis fast asleep in the matching set of pink and white pajamas. Nakia walked inside her room and placed Lexis' comforter over her before kissing the top of her head and walking out of the room. Nakia was pleased when she walked back into her living room, and it was spotless.

"See sis, I told you Uncle Jay had it. How was work?" Jalyn asked, as he walked out the kitchen.

"Bro, that shit was crazy. It's some young ass girls at the hotel who might be getting' pimped out by this grown ass nigga. They wanna call the police on him, but I don't know how I feel about that. The mother in me wants to make sure them babies get out that situation, but the street bitch in me don't speak Pig Latin."

"How do you know they young, and what makes you think he pimpin' them out?"

"You can look at them and tell they are just babies. One of them can't be no more than fourteen or fifteen," Nakia sighed.

"Hell nah, Kia, stay outta that shit. It don't have nothing to do with you. Imma tell you now, he ain't workin' by himself. It's always a bigger fish, and that's the muthafucka you don't want to fuck with."

"Bailey made a good point today. She asked me if it was one of our daughters, wouldn't we want someone to help them? I know for a fact if it was Lexis out there, I would want someone to help her," Nakia replied.

"But it ain't Lexi. You don't know what the fuck is really going on. Look, if them old ass ladies at yo job want to call the police, let them do it. But you stay out that shit, you got yo own kids to worry about. Snitches get stitches and end up in ditches, remember that."

Nakia nodded her head, knowing her brother was right; however, something in her heart wouldn't allow her to just let this go. Nakia had grown up in the hood, so she knew the code of the streets. However, she felt like when it came to children, that shit was off limits.

CHAPTER SEVEN

Tianna stood there, anger seeping through her pores as she looked at her battered body in the mirror. She had an open gash at the start of her hairline from where Russell had hit her with his gun. A busted lip, two black eyes, and a host of other bruises and scratches. Causing her to cry from her own refection. *I can't believe that nigga did this to me*, she thought to herself as she held a washcloth under warm water. She placed the towel on her face in an effort to clean herself and winced from the pain. She was sure she had at least a few broken ribs from the constant kicks to her midsection, however, there was no way she was going to the hospital. Hospitals brought police, and that wasn't the route she was going. So, instead, Tianna popped two Tylenols and chased them with the water from her bathroom sink.

It was at that very moment that Tianna knew she would do whatever she could to get the fuck away from Russell. She came up with a plan to take his clientele. She would charge less money for the same service. There was no way the dudes wouldn't all flock to her. If she could get a few girls on her team, she could build her own business and take Russell down in the process.

The hatred she now felt for Russell ran deep, and she was ready to fuck him up. Anyone who knew Russell knew his money was the closest thing to him. So, Tianna was gonna hit him where it hurt. I promise this will be the last time he puts his hands on me. I'll kill his ass next time.

Russell pulled up at the Days Inn with both Hannah and Nikki in his SUV. The rooms were much cheaper at that hotel, plus the rooms were outside. Which made it much easier to access, seeing how there was no lobby to walk through. He knew Tianna would be out of commission for a few days, so he only needed three rooms. Once the rooms were rented, the three of them went to get settled in and start working. With Tianna being gone, Russell knew Nikki and Hannah would have to do double the work in order to keep the money good. Russell sat on the bed and kicked his shoes off. Just thinking about the money he might lose made him want to get back in his truck and go beat the shit out of Tianna again. He knew he needed something to calm him down, so he pulled his phone out his pocket and called Hannah.

"Hannah, come in my room and holla at me for a minute."

"Okay, I'm on my way," Hannah replied before ending the call.

Two minutes later, Hannah was knocking at Russell's room door. He opened it and invited her in before sitting back on the bed. There were no words that needed to be spoken, they both knew why she was there. Russell unzipped his pants and pulled his manhood through the opening in his boxers. Hannah dropped to her knees in front of him and took him into her mouth, sucking and slurping, as Russell closed his eyes and moaned.

"That's right baby, get all the nut out for daddy. Suck that shit," Russell moaned.

Hannah did one more lap around the head of Russell's dick, and he couldn't take it any longer. He shot warm cum down Hannah's throat, and she swallowed every drop. Spent, Russell laid back on the bed breathing heavily.

"You always know how to get daddy back right. That was just what

I needed. Go get yoself together. I'm bout to login and set y'all up some jobs. It's grind time, baby, so I know y'all ready."

Once Hannah was out the room, Russell pulled out his phones and logged into his website. He'd just opened up for business when one of his phones rung. Looking down at it, he saw it was his brother Travis.

"What up doe, bro?" Russell spoke into the phone.

"Shit, I just been chillin'. Got some shit on the floor for you doe."

"Talk to me nice," Russell replied.

"It's this little bitch I met that's tryin' to get down with yo shit. Her name is Shamia, and she bad. Lil young bitch, down for anything."

"Where you know her from? How old is she?" Russell asked.

"I been seein' her in the hood for the past few months. Only been talkin' to her for a couple weeks though. She nineteen, hoe say she ready to get money. I told her I know a guy that's getting' the type of money she's tryin' to get," Travis replied.

"You got a picture of her?"

"Yeah, I'm bout to send it to you know."

Russell held the phone as he waited on Travis to send the attachments. Once his phone vibrated, he knew he'd reserved them. When he opened up his text thread, he saw the thickest chocolate bitch he'd ever seen. His dick hardened at her plump behind and thick thighs.

"Can you get her over to me today so I can see what's up with her?" Russell asked.

"Yeah, I'm sure I can. Let me just call her and make sure."

"Cool, hit me back and let me know what's up."

Russell took call after call, sending all the jobs to his girls as he waited on Travis to call him back. It had been over an hour, and he still hadn't let him know if thick ass Miss Chocolate will be down to come for an interview. Finally, his phone rung and it was Travis. He let Russell know he would be on his way once he sent the address. Russell wanted to get to the money, and he knew a thick ass bitch on his roster would bring him even more of it. He just hoped she was down the way Travis said she was.

Travis texted twenty minutes later to let Russell know they were outside. He opened the room door and watched as Miss Chocolate sashayed her way to his door. Russell was mesmerized by the way her hips swayed with each step. Damn I never had a bitch like this before.

"Shamia, this is my brother Russell," Travis introduced as the two of them walked into the room.

Shamia, who Russell had already nicknamed Miss Chocolate, was more beautiful in person than she was in the picture Travis had sent. She was wearing a green and black sundress, which accentuated every one of her curves. Her hair was up in a high ponytail that hung down to her ass. Every baby hair was laid to perfection. Her hands were neatly manicured with medium length French tips, small Swarovski crystals adorned every other fingernail. Her makeup was applied perfectly as if a professional had done it. She was indeed flawless, however, what took the cake was when Russell looked down and her open toed sandals revealed all white toes.

"Hi Russell, it's nice to meet you finally. I been telling yo brother for days now that I'm trying to work. He been sleepin' on me though, like I ain't no money maker." Shamia boasted.

"I'll be the judge of all that, I see you got the look, but can you fuck? What's gonna make these niggas keep coming back to you?" Russell asked.

Without a word, Shamia grabbed his hand and led him to the bed. She pulled the straps of her sundress down, exposing her supple breasts, before turning to look at Travis.

"Can you give us a minute? I need to let this nigga know why he needs me on his team."

Travis nodded and exited the room, closing the door behind him. Russell watched as Shamia got completely naked in front of him. Russell was in complete awe and wanted nothing more than to see if her body was as soft as it looked.

"Tell me what u like, daddy," Shamia posed.

"Show me what that mouth do."

Shamia obliged, dropping down to her knees in front of him and grabbing his rock-hard manhood. Cupping his balls with her free hand, she spit on the head of his penis. Shamia picked up her pace as she dangled his balls with her fingers. All the work she put in had Russell moaning like a little bitch. Once the head of his shaft swelled, Shamia knew that he was close to his climax. She removed his manhood from her mouth and looked into his eyes.

"Hand me the condom so I can put it on you," Shamia instructed.

Russell grabbed a Magnum off the nightstand and quickly handed it to Shamia. Ripping the wrapper open with her teeth, she placed it on her tongue. Shamia put the tip of her tongue on the head of Russell's dick and used her lips to roll the condom onto him. His eyes widened in disbelief. Russell had never had anyone put a condom on him in that way before and it sent him over the edge.

"Lay back, I wanna ride this dick," Shamia commanded, rolling the tip of her tongue across her top lip.

Russell obliged, and Shamia climbed on top, straddling him. He gripped her ass cheeks, and his manhood slid into her. That was all she wrote, they fucked until they couldn't fuck anymore. Both out of breath when they finished.

"You start tonight. Go home and get yourself together. Pack up a few things, then come back," Russell stated.

Shamia smiled confidently. She knew from the moment she walked into the room that she was going to get the job. She nodded her head in satisfaction ready to get to the money.

"Go get Travis and tell him to come holla at me for a minute."

"Okay, I'll see you later," Shamia said, walking out the door.

A few moments later, Travis entered the room. Travis stood about six foot five inches tall, with a very muscular build. His dark skin and low haircut had everyone in the neighborhood comparing him to rapper Meek Mill. Travis wasn't involved in Russell's business at all. He just wasn't the type to pimp out any bitch. However, he was the type to make money.

"Look bro, I wanna bring you in on my business. These hoes have been getting out of line, and as I bring in more, I don't know if I can handle it all myself."

"Bring me in how? Russell, I'm never one to knock yo hustle, but this ain't my field," Travis stated.

"Yeah, I know. That's why I wanna bring you in as security. You don't have to let me know your answer now, just think about it and let me know in a few days."

"Fasho, I can do that. I'll hit u up tomorrow with my answer."

Nakia walked into work feeling well rested on Monday morning. Her weekend had been the quick reset she'd needed to take on another work week. Walking into the back office to clock in, she saw Bailey and Anastasia talking.

"Good morning y'all," She greeted.

"Good morning, Nakia, you look happy today," Bailey stated.

"Yeah, I am. I had a restful weekend."

"Well, that's good. Work had been busy this morning, but no crazy people so far, so that's a good thing. Oh, and your friends from the third floor left," Anastasia announced.

Nakia was happy to hear they were gone. She'd been going back and forth about notifying the police about what was going on. However, with them being gone, she would no longer have to worry about it. It was out of her hands. She was more than happy that everything had worked out. Smiling, Nakia walked back to the front desk and started her work day.

Surprisingly, the day went by smoothly, and before Nakia new it, it was five o'clock and Shelby was walking in ready to release Nakia from her shift. She clocked out and headed to her car, ready to go home, cook dinner, and relax with her children. Nakia had just merged onto 94 when her phone rung.

"Hello?' Nakia answered through her earbuds.

"Hey girl, what you doing?" Nakia's best friend, Simone, asked.

"Girl nothing, just leaving work. What you up to?"

"Nothing much, just seeing what you were doing. I got a bottle of wine and wanted to know if u wanted to share it with me," Simone inquired.

"I'm always down for a good glass of wine, girl. I should be home in about ten minutes," Nakia informed.

"Cool, I'll be there in thirty," Simone said before ending the call.

Soon as she got home, Nakia changed out of her work clothes and began dinner. She'd just put the chicken breasts in the pan when there was a knock at the door. Knowing it was Simone, Nakia called out, telling her to come in.

"Hey boo! How u doing on this cold afternoon?" Simone asked cheerfully.

"I know it's cold as hell out there, ain't it? I'm good, just trying to cook up this dinner for these kids," Nakia replied.

"Awe shit, I done came over at the right time. What you cookin'?"

Nakia ran down the menu to Simone and her mouth watered with every item Nakia called out. Everyone that knew Nakia knew she was a beast in the kitchen, and Simone definitely was going to stay for dinner.

"Where my niece and nephew at?" Simone asked.

"Upstairs waiting on me to finish cookin'. Girl, them kids act like they be starving when they get home from school," Nakia replied, laughing.

"Let me go say hi to them, then we can pop this bottle because I got some shit to tell you."

Nakia pulled two wine glasses from her cabinet and continued to cook as she waited on Simone to return. Nakia could only imagine what she had to tell her. Knowing her best friend, however, Nakia knew it was about a guy.

"Girl, them kids funny as hell. And why you didn't tell me Shaud made the basketball team at his school? I told him I would be at his game on Saturday," Simone announced.

"Girl, I thought I did, but so much be going on that it must have slipped my mind. Anyway girl, what is it that you got to tell me?"

"So, bitch, do you remember that guy Zeke I met a couple months ago? Well, I been seein' him a little more regularly now. Bitch he took me to Miami for the weekend. And I'm not talkin' about just me and him. We ate the finest cuisine at every meal, and he took me on a fifteen thousand dollar shoppin' spree. Nakia, my ass is in love."

"Bitch, yo ass is always in love, this ain't nothing knew," Nakia teased, laughing.

She poured herself a glass of wine and sat at her kitchen table with Simone while she waited for the potatoes to boil.

"Nah, I'm in love for real this time. Did you hear what I just said this nigga did? Not to mention he got the best dick I've ever had in my fuckin' life. Bitch I'm bout to settle down and have all the babies this nigga wants."

"Girl what? You talkin' crazy now. I ain't never heard you talking about havin' no kids. Now this nigga got you wanting to be barefoot and pregnant. He must have a magic dick."

"I ain't say anything about being barefoot. Imma still be in heels, pregnant and all. Don't play with me," Simone joked.

"Real talk, if you happy then I'm happy. I just wanna know when can I meet this man that got you glowin' like this?"

"Next week at my birthday dinner, y'all both gonna be there," Simone replied.

"Cool, I can't wait. I got to see the daddy of my future nieces and nephews that I thought would never be here," Nakia chuckled.

Simone stayed and had a nice home cooked meal with Nakia and her family. They had polished off the bottle of wine over a few laughs, and Simone had even stayed and helped with the dinner dishes. Once everything was cleaned and the children were asleep in their beds, Nakia went up to her room and smoked her nightly blunt before falling asleep herself.

CHAPTER EIGHT

Over the next few months business had been booming for Russell. His brother Travis had come on as his security, and they had even upgraded from hotel rooms to a six-bedroom Airbnb. Tianna had come back to work, and he'd even added three more girls to his roster. Kendra, who was 21, was the oldest girl Russell had. She was short, standing on four foot eleven inches tall. She was caramel complected, and although she didn't have much ass back there, she had some of the biggest titties Russell had ever seen. There were also Strawberry and Cream, a set of twins that Russell couldn't get enough off. Cream was a light skinned beauty with skin as soft as whipped cream, hence the name. Strawberry had the same light skin, with curly hair as red as a strawberry. They did everything together, giving their johns the ultimate pleasure, so Russell gave them the nickname strawberry and cream. Business was good, and Russell couldn't be happier.

"Russell, I think we have a problem," Travis announced, walking into the living room where Russell was seated.

"What's up, bro?"

"I think Tianna is stealing our clientele and doing some side gigs. I came across this website. I know the names are different, but unless this bitch got a twin out here, this is her," Travis handed Russell his phone.

Russell scrolled through, looking at the many pictures that were posted of her. As he looked through the services and prices, he found that Tianna was offering the same exact services he was but at a lower price. Fury shot through his entire body as he stood to his feet.

"This bitch has lost her fuckin' mind. See, I tried to be nice but this hoe ain't getting' it. I put hands on the bitch twice and thought that was enough for her to fall in line. But no, I see Imma have to make an example out of this bitch!" Russell yelled.

"What you wanna do?" Travis asked.

"That bitch tryin' to play with my fuckin' money, I got something for that bitch. Pretend to be a john and set up a date with that hoe," Russell said as he exited the living room.

About an hour later both Travis and Russell were on their way to the spot Tianna was working out of. They pulled into the driveway of a small house which Russell knew was an Airbnb. Damn, this bitch has stolen my entire setup, Russell thought to himself. The two men got out the car and walked up to the door, ringing the doorbell. When Tianna opened the door, her eyes widened at the sight of Russell and Travis. Her heart dropped to the pit of her stomach because she knew she'd been caught. She tried to slam the door in their faces but was too slow. Travis had already blocked the door with his foot and was now pushing his way in. Tianna screamed as his force caused her to fall to the floor.

"Please y'all, don't hurt me. It's not what it looks like," Tianna pleaded.

"It's not what it looks like? It looks like yo ass is tryin' to fuck up my business. See, this right here is what we call a conflict of interest. You went and started your own business, doing the exact same thing I do, and became my competition. Now what you think I should do to you for that?" Russell asked.

"Nah, Russell, you got it all wrong, I told you it ain't what it look like. I wasn't tryin' to fuck up yo business, daddy, I was tryin' to bring you more. I thought that if I was to bring you more people, then you would see that I was yo real bottom bitch," Tianna boasted.

Russell laughed out loud and turned to look at Travis. "You hear this shit nigga, now the bitch was tryin' to send me more clients."

"So not only was you takin' money out my pockets, but you gonna look me in my face and lie? You just fuckin' up more and more Tianna."

"Please, Russell, I'm not lying. I was just trying to make you some money."

"You was trying to make me some money huh? Well, why didn't you just say that? Come on, since you wanna make me some money, let's go make some," Russell stated.

Tianna looked up at Russell confused. Was she hearing him right? Was he really okay with this? Tianna cautiously got up off the floor and looked at Russell. Surprised that he didn't look mad at all. Maybe he does believe my story. Let me just go back to the house with him and go to work so he don't get mad. I definitely don't need another ass whippin'. That shit had me laid up for weeks, Tianna thought.

She gathered a few things and walked out to the car with Russell and Travis. Happy that she had gotten out of things so lightly, she placed her bag in the trunk before getting into the backseat.

"Imma drive bro, toss me the keys," Russell said.

Once they'd been driving for about fifteen minutes, Tianna noticed they were not driving in the direction of Russell's Airbnb.

"Where we going Russell, you got a new spot or something?" She asked.

Russell didn't reply, instead he just kept driving. Tianna knew Russell was the type that hated being asked questions, so when he didn't reply, she sat back in her seat without another word. When they pulled into the parking lot of the Velvet Rope strip club, Tianna was even more confused than ever. What the fuck are we doing here? She wondered.

"Get out the car," Russell commanded.

"You want me to dance for you, daddy?" Tianna asked, retrieving her bag from the trunk.

"You said you was tryin' to make me a lot of money, right?" Russell asked.

"Yes daddy, all this has ever been about is makin' you money. I just wanna be your top earner, daddy."

"Good, I was just makin' sure that's what you said. Come on in here, this where the real money is," Russell stated.

The three of them walked into the club and was greeted by the short Albanian woman who sat behind a small desk.

"Russell, is that you?" Rosa asked, standing from her seat.

"Oh my God, it is. Where have you been? My dad asked about you just the other day. We thought you had taken your business elsewhere," she continued.

"Yeah, I know it's been a minute. I would never take my business anywhere else; your family has been very good to me. I just haven't had any business to bring your father's way... until now," Russell said, pointing over at Tianna.

"Ohhh, she's pretty," Rose complimented as she eyed Tianna up and down.

"Is your father here?"

"Yes, he's in his office. Go ahead back there, I'll let him know you're coming."

Russell nodded and both Travis and Tianna followed him through the club. Once in the back, they went through a set of double doors which lead to a staircase. Russell knocked at the door that was at the top of the stairs. A old white haired man holding a cigar stood behind the door.

"Russell, when Rosa told me you were on your way up, I thought she was joking with me. How the hell have you been?"

"I've been good Fatbar, how about yourself?"

"I'm better now that you're here. Seeing you means I'm about to be seeing a lot of money," Fatbar replied.

"Yeah, you know how we get down. Her name is Tianna."

Fatbar smiled as he looked Tianna over. She smiled back at him as well. Taking a step closer to her, he ran his liver spotted hand along her breasts. Before telling her to turn around and grabbing her ass. Tianna was used to old ugly men touching her, but this felt more like an examination. Tianna began to feel uncomfortable and couldn't wait for this to be over.

"She's tight and young. How much you asking?" Fatbar asked.

"Thirty," Russell replied.

Fatbar gave Tianna the once over for the last time before he nodded his head. Tianna watched in confusion as Fatbar walked over to the safe on his wall and opened it, handing Russell a stack of money.

"See what I mean, every time I see you, I make money. The thirty thousand I just handed you is nothing compared to the profit I'm going to make once she gets to Albania. Tell me something, why did you sell her so cheap?"

Sell me? Albania? Wait a fuckin' minute? What the fuck is goin' on? Tianna's heart began pounding in her chest. She looked around the room, searching for a way to escape. Russell had lost his mind if he thought he would just sell her to someone like she was a fucking slave or a piece of property. She began backing up towards the door slowly because there was no way she was going out without a fight.

"The bitch been getting out of pocket, and I have to make an example out of this hoe. She tried to become my competition by doing her own hoein' on the side. You know the punishment for that, Fatbar."

Fatbar nodded his head, knowing exactly what Russell was saying. Tianna was almost to the door when Travis grabbed her arm and pulled her closer to him.

"This bitch tryin' to get away." Travis announced.

"She wouldn't have gotten far even if she did get out that door. I got way too much security around," Fatbar said

Tears started falling from her eyes and she pleaded with Russell not to let this happen. She knew she'd fucked up by trickin' without his knowledge, however, selling her to a trafficking ring was too much.

"Russell, wait, please don't do this. I won't do it anymore, I promise. Please just don't do this."

"Bitch it's already done. You don't wanna do it? Buy yourself from Fatbar if that's the case. You're his property now, so it's nothing I can do about it," Russell stated coldly.

Tianna screamed as she watched Russell and Travis walk out the door. She would have never gone against Russell if she knew it would end up like this. Being sold like a slave to a sex ring in a foreign country was never in the job description. Tianna wasn't having it, and she didn't see any other way out other than to fight. If Russell was going to sell her, it would be at her own will. With that, Tianna jumped on Russell's back and began punching him in the head. Being caught off guard, it took Russell a few seconds to realize what was happening. Once he did, Russell tossed Tianna off of him like she was a rag doll. She hit the floor with a thud, and Russell and Travis resumed walking out the door.

"Yo ass is crazy, why you toss her off you like that? I know that shit had to hurt. And did you hear the way she screamed when we walked out that door?" Travis laughed. "When you going back to get her?"

"I'm not going to get that bitch, she goin' to Albania to work for them. I'm not playin' with no bitches no more," Russell replied.

"Wait, so you really leavin' her here? Do you know what they gonna do to her in that foreign country?" Travis countered, stunned by the coldhearted actions of his brother.

"Yeah, I know exactly what they gonna do to her. She didn't want to play by my rules, cool. Now her ass gonna be working for pennies until she either makes enough to buy herself out of it or dies in the process. Either way, fuck that bitch. I'm not playing with none of these hoes no more," Russell countered.

Once back at the house, Russell made sure all his girls had dates lined up for at least the next two hours. He needed to have everyone occupied so he could have some time for himself. He hated that he'd had to get rid of Tianna because he really liked her. However, what she'd done could not go without consequence. From that moment on, he was putting his foot the fuck down and would no longer be ran over. If these bitches were not going to respect him as Daddy, they would be sold to the highest bidder.

He walked into his room and immediately grab the blunt in his ashtray and lit it. He let the smoke invade his lungs as he picked up his phone and scrolled through Instagram. He needed to find some more girls, and since he'd found Nikki on IG, he decided to try his luck again. Russell scrolled through dozens of pictures, liking some and following others. He even sent out a few DMs to the girls that looked like they would be down to work. Once he was done, Russell got in the shower and made an effort to wash away the stress from the day.

Nakia stood in her bathroom looking at herself in the mirror, and she had to admit, she cleaned up rather well. She normally didn't go out, however, after having such a good time at Simone's party, she decided to treat herself to a night out at least once a month. All she did was work and spend time with her children, so adult time was much needed. She dressed in a tight black dress, which accentuated every curve she had. She flat ironed her hair bone straight and placed a part down the middle. She looked stunning if she did say so herself.

Once she was dressed, she kissed her children and let Jalyn know she wouldn't be back until the club closed. Jalyn didn't mind watching his niece and nephew whenever Nakia needed him to, so he was happy to spend time with them. He was even happier that Nakia was finally starting to enjoy life again. He'd seen firsthand how the death of her children's father had affected her, and although he knew the pain would never completely go away, he was happy she was starting to heal.

Nakia pulled into the parking lot of Views and sent Simone a text, letting her know she was there. Simone, who was already inside, let Nakia know to just come in. Nakia scanned the dimly lit bar and spotted her friend sitting at a table with two men. She knew one to be Zeke, Simone's boyfriend. However, the other man was not a familiar face.

"Hey girl, we just placed an order for some lamb chops. I ordered enough for you because I know how much you love them," Simone stated.

Nakia smiled and nodded her head before taking a seat.

"Nakia, this is Zeke's friend, Raphael," Simone introduced.

Nakia held out her hand for him to shake as she greeted him before taking her seat. The four of them sat around the table, eating, drinking, and listening to the music the DJ was playing.

"So, Nakia, Simone told me you were single and looking for a new friend. I knew when she said that I had to introduce you to Raphael," Zeke stated.

Nakia almost choked on her damn lamb chop once she heard those words. Not one time did she realize this was supposed to be a set up.

She looked over at Simone, and if looks could kill, Simone would've been DOA. Nakia was pissed. She thought the least Simone could have done was tell her what was going on instead of blindsiding her.

"Excuse me for a moment, I have to go to that lady's room. Simone, why don't you join me?" Nakia suggested.

"Sure, come on."

Nakia all but dragged Simone to the bathroom, as she tried to get out of Zeke's and Raphael's line of sight. Once they were in the bathroom Nakia let lose.

"Are you fuckin' serious, Simone? Why wouldn't you tell me he was coming? First off, I don't like blind dates, and you know that. Secondly, here I am thinkin' we about to have some casual girl time, and we can't even have girl talk because it's two men at the table. What the fuck is this shit, Simone?" Nakia asked, clearly upset by what her friend had done.

"Nakia, relax, you need to live a little. You act like it's something wrong with meeting people. Zeke wanted to see me tonight, but I told him I already had plans with you. I knew how excited you were about our night out, and I didn't want to cancel. So, instead, I told him to bring a friend. It's just a friendly little dinner date. His father also owns the Velvet Rope, so can you say money?"

Nakia rolled her eyes. She was never one to be concerned about how much money a man had because she made her own. She wasn't a gold digger like Simone, so those types of things didn't move her. In reality, Nakia didn't know if she was ready to date anyone. She was still grieving the loss of her children's father. Simone knew that firsthand. So, that was all the more reason why Nakia couldn't understand why she had done this.

"Simone, I'm going home."

"Wait, what? Girl, come on, don't do that. We just having a few drinks and eatin' some good ass lamb chops. Why you gonna go home and ruin your night out? You need this, we both know that," Simone pointed out.

Nakia just looked at her friend, looking at her with those big eyes that Nakia just couldn't say no to.

"Alright bitch, I'll stay. But not because you asked me to, but because I look too damn good in this dress to just go home," Nakia laughed before they walked out the bathroom and back to their table.

"Is everything alright?" Zeke asked once they were back at the table.

"Yes, everything is fine. Why don't we order another round of drinks?" Simone offered, signaling for the waitress.

After a few drinks, Nakia let loose and finally began to have a good time. She found that Raphael worked at a tech company and also helped his father with his club on the weekends. Raphael didn't have to work for anyone, however, he wanted to be his own man and not piggy-back off of daddy's money. Nakia admired that because she was the same way. Anything Nakia wanted or needed was solely up to her to obtain. She was happy she stayed at the bar because Raphael was turning out to be a cool guy. By the end of the night, they had exchanged numbers and was looking forward to seeing each other again.

"What do you mean we can't extend?" Russell yelled furiously into the phone.

"I'm sorry, sir, but the house was already rented for today months ago, there is nothing I can do. You are more than welcome to book the home for any dates that it is available. However, I need you to vacate by noon so the cleaning staff can go in," the woman on the phone said.

"Fine," Russell stated before hanging up.

Russell walked to each girl and told them to pack their belongings before heading to his own room. He sat on the bed and searched the Airbnb app in an effort to find another place to stay. He searched house after house, and there was nothing. Everything was either too small, too far, or unavailable. He didn't want to go back to the hotel, however, that seemed to be his only option. Going onto the Priceline app on his phone, he booked four rooms at the Courtyard Marriot.

CHAPTER NINE

"Girl, you not gonna believe who's back," Bailey spoke, running down to the front desk.

"Umm, I give up, who's back?" Nakia asked.

"That sex trafficker! But this time, he's with four girls, and they all look young. Why the fuck would he come back here? We gotta take him down for real this time, girl. He cannot get away with this."

Nakia looked at Bailey confused. What did she think they could do other than call the police? It wasn't their job to take anyone down, it was the polices', and clearly, Nakia was the only one who seemed to know that.

"How do you know it's him?" Nakia asked.

"I saw him. He's back on the third floor, I just don't know what room. I swear, if I see any strange activity, I'm calling the police."

About fifteen minutes later, Nakia watched as the young white girl she remembered from last time walk out into the lobby. She watched as the girl walked into the vestibule and stood there like she was waiting on someone. When a car pulled up, the girl walked out and got inside. The car pulled out the parking lot and went on its way. Not even five minutes later, Nakia saw the other young girl walk into the lobby with two other girls who seemed to be twins. They whispered a few words to each other before two cars pulled up and the girls left. Nakia spent the rest of her shift watching as all four of the girls repeated the same cycle three more times. Getting into cars, pulling off, and getting dropped back off about forty-five minutes later.

"Bitch, I think what Bailey was sayin' about that guy traffickin' them girls is true. I've watched them girls get in and out of cars all day, and did she tell you it's two more with them? And bitch, they wearing these skimpy ass outfits with tons of make-up on trying to look grown or some shit. Where are their parents at?" Nakia questioned, rushing to the back office. She was trying to mind her own business, but the more she watched the girls, the more she thought about her own children.

"See, Bailey called it," Anastasia replied.

"I called what?" Bailey asked, overhearing her name in their conversation.

"That something was going on with that guy and those young girls. Nakia has seen them getting in and out of cars all day, same way you did," Anastasia confirmed.

"See, I told you!" Bailey exclaimed with wide eyes.

Bailey's mother's intuition was right on the money. She knew that man had those girls selling their bodies, same way she knew they were young. The man was clearly manipulating those little girls. Bailey never had a daughter, as a mother of two sons, she always prayed for a little girl. However, it didn't happen until she was blessed with her first grandchild, a little girl who Bailey cherished. The same way that she would protect her granddaughter was going to be the same way she protected the little girls in that room.

"If they are still here tomorrow, I'm calling the police. It's so sad seeing those young girls out here like this," Bailey continued.

"I don't think you should wait until tomorrow; this is crazy. I think you should call them right now," Anastasia spoke.

"No, I'll wait. But if they're here tomorrow, I'm calling."

The rest of the day went by slowly. Nakia had two hours left of her shift, and she couldn't wait to clock out. It seemed like every guest had gotten on her nerves today, and all she wanted to do was curl up in her bed with a glass of wine and Netflix. She had just taken a seat when an elderly woman walked up to the desk.

"Hello, how can I help you?" Nakia greeted, standing from her chair.

"Is there an ice machine on this floor? I've looked everywhere and can't seem to find it," the woman stated as she looked down at the ice bucket she was holding.

"Yes, there is, it's one straight through that middle hallway to the left," Nakia replied with a smile.

The woman nodded her head, and as soon as she walked off, the phone rang. Nakia answered it in her polite professional voice, all the while rolling her eyes. Once she was done making the reservation, she disconnected the call and walked back to her seat. She'd just sat down when the same elderly woman walked back up to the desk.

"I just can't find that ice machine," she stated, still holding an empty ice bucket.

Nakia wanted to scream. Damn, is this bitch blind? I just told her where the ice machine was, Nakia thought to herself. She cocked a half smile and told the old woman to follow her, as she guided her through the hallway and around the corner to the ice machine. The woman thanked Nakia, and Nakia walked back up to the desk, only to find a guest standing there waiting on her return.

"Hello, how can I help you?" Nakia asked, noticing it was the creepy guy who they thought was pimping out the young girls.

"Hello, I'm a guest here. I have four rooms on the third floor. The Wi-Fi up there is hella slow, and I was wondering if I can change my rooms," Russell stated with a smile.

"Let me see what I can do," Nakia said, as she scrolled through the available rooms on the computer. "Okay, it looks like we have four rooms right by each other, 105, 106, 107, and 108. They are close to the router, so the Wi-Fi should be faster," Nakia stated.

"Is that on the first floor?" He asked.

"Yes, it is, and right next to the router. That way, you won't have any more trouble with the Wi-Fi," Nakia replied.

Russell looked at Nakia a few moments, like he was in deep thought before he replied.

"Is there anywhere else you can put us? I would rather not be on the first floor."

"Yes, we have other rooms, but those four rooms are the closest to the router. I can't guarantee fast Wi-Fi in any other room but those."

Russell let out a long breath. He had already cased the hotel and knew that except for by the elevators, they only had cameras on the first floor. The last thing Russell wanted to do was get caught on camera with his underaged hoes. There was no way he was taking those four rooms, Wi-Fi be damned.

"Do you have four rooms on the second floor that's next to each other?" Russell asked.

Nakia searched through the system in an effort to assist her guest.

"I don't have four rooms side by side, but I can give you some that's close to each other, with just a few rooms in-between," she stated.

"Nah, that won't work," Russell replied, shaking his head.

"Well, I'm sorry, sir, if you don't want the four rooms on the first floor, then that's the closest I can get you to the router."

"Those rooms are not close enough to each other, and I don't want to change floors. You don't have anything else on the same floor I'm on now that might be right above the router?"

"You just asked me if I had rooms on the second floor," Nakia looked at Russell skeptically before she continued. "The rooms you have would be the ones above the router."

Russell rubbed his thumb and index finger over his chin several times as if he was in deep thought again. Nakia couldn't help but shake her head in annoyance. What is so hard about the damn decision? He's the one that came down wanting to be close to the router. I can't wait to get off and away from this place, she thought to herself.

"See the problem is, I'm in a poly relationship and all four of my girls got a lot of stuff. I do want to be close to the router, but I don't want to have to move all that stuff from floor to floor, you feel me? You know how you women are, y'all can't just travel with just one bag like normal people. And my ass got four bitches, so you can only imagine all the shit they got," Russell tried to persuade Nakia.

"Whoa, you sayin' way too much. So, you gonna stay in those same rooms?" Nakia asked, not wanting to take the conversation any further.

"My bad, I know you probably didn't want to hear all that. And yes, we will be stayin' in the rooms we already have," Russell chucked before walking away.

Nakia just shook her head before taking her seat. I wish time would hurry up and pass, so it will be time for me to go home. These guests are getting on my damn nerves.

"Girl, we need to call homeland right now! Come look out the back door," Bailey stated, as she motioned Nakia to follow her.

Nakia watched as the young girl walked the parking lot in a black and red two-piece skirt set. She had on a pair of black open toed shoes that strapped up to her thigh. It was all of forty degrees outside and she was walking around in next to nothing. Nakia just couldn't take it anymore. It hurt her heart knowing the girl couldn't have been more than fifteen years old, if that.

"See, I told you he was pimping them little girls out. We need to call Homeland right now," Bailey pushed, as she walked back towards the office, with Nakia following close behind.

Nakia didn't want to get involved with anything regarding the police, however, she had young children herself. She knew if either one of her children were ever in a predicament such as this one, she would want someone to help them. With that, she did the only thing she could do, found the number to Homeland Security.

"Detective Johnson, Homeland Security," the officer answered on the third ring.

"Hello, Detective Johnson. This is Nakia from the Courtyard Marriott by the airport. I'm calling because we have noticed some suspicious activity with a few of the guests here, and we would like someone to come check it out."

"Okay, it's good that you called us. What seems to be the activity that you have witnessed?" The Detective asked.

"There is a man staying in the hotel room with four girls that seem to be young. I'm talking underage young. They are walking around very scantily dressed and we are almost sure he is making these girls sell themselves to men. I mean, I can look in their faces and tell they are very young. Maybe between fourteen and sixteen," Nakia stated.

"What's the name, address, and phone number of the registered guest?" The Detective asked.

After Nakia gave him all the necessary information, the Detective told her he would be at the hotel within the next twenty minutes before ending the call.

"What did he say?" Bailey asked.

"He's gonna be here in about twenty minutes."

"Who's gonna be here?" Anastasia asked, as she walked into the back office.

"Homeland security. We just called them on that guy on the third floor," Bailey replied.

"Good, cuz his shady ass definitely got something going on with them girls. I just seen him in the parking lot yelling at the white girl. He cocked his hand back like he was going to hit her and everything. Then when she started crying, he busted out laughing. He's an asshole," Anastasia stated.

"He's a sex trafficker, and he is pimping out them little girls is what he is," Bailey said.

Just as promised, within twenty minutes, Detective Johnson was walking through the door with his partner who was introduced as Detective Hampton. Anastasia brought them to the back office where Nakia and Bailey were sitting. They both shook their hands before taking a seat and asking them to recall everything they saw. By the time Nakia and Bailey were done, the Detectives were calling for back up and ready to get in position to take Russell down.

"What's going on?" Shelby asked, as she walked through the hotel entrance.

"Homeland is about to arrest the weird guy on the third floor for trafficking. It's been crazy here today," Anastasia explained.

Shelby stood there with her mouth hung open, as if she couldn't believe what was being told to her. She immediately placed her lunchbox and purse down in her office and walked out to the front desk where she would have a good view of the lobby. Just as the task force was starting to take their positions, two of the young girls walked into the lobby. The white girl leading the way as the black girl followed.

"That's two of them right there," Anastasia whispered.

With that, both Detectives Johnson and Hampton walked over to them. The Detectives were dressed in plain clothes, so initially neither Hannah nor Nikki knew they were cops. When they spoke to the girls, Hannah began licking her lips and twirling her hair through her fingers. She was always working no matter what, and if she sensed a potential john then she was gonna make sure she made the first move before any other hoe did. She was damn near a master at the game.

"How can I help you two fine lookin' gentleman?" Hannah asked sexily.

"Do you two have some identification on you?" Detective Johnson asked.

"What? What kind of question is that? I'm not showing you shit; I don't even fuckin' know you. Fuck I look like," Hannah spat.

Nikki, however, didn't say a word, as she looked around the lobby. There was a woman standing in front of the main entrance and what seemed like the entire staff standing behind the front desk. What made it even more noticeable was the fact they were all starring at them. Nikki knew when something wasn't right, and this was one of those moments.

"It's the cops," Nikki whispered.

Detective Hampton looked over at Nikki and smiled. "Yes, we are Detectives with a task force, and we are just here to help. Are you two in any danger? If you are, we will get you out of it, but you have to talk to us."

"Oh, hell no, I don't have to say shit to y'all. I know my rights, and we didn't do anything wrong," Hannah said, turning on her heels, with Nikki right behind her.

"Ma'am please, we just want to help," Detective Hampton called out as he began to follow after the two girls.

"Let it go, Hampton, it's him we want. Let's just go up to the room. Everyone is already in position, they're just waiting on us," Detective Johnson said.

He nodded at his partner, as the two of them walked over to

the elevator. Detective Hampton took one last look at the two girls who were now standing outside the back entrance in what seemed to be deep conversation. After fifteen years on the job, he knew trouble when he saw it, and the two of them were definitely deep in it. He wished they would have just talked to him because once he took down their pimp, they would most likely have nowhere to go. It saddened him how grown men would just manipulate young girls into doing whatever little nasty thing their fucked up minds desired.

When the elevator stopped on the third floor, both officers walked down the hall cautiously with their hands on their guns. When they made it to the room, Johnson knocked on the door and waited several second before a voice asked who it was.

"This is Detective Johnson and my partner Detective Hampton, and we have a couple of questions for you."

Russell's eyes widened in shock. What the fuck were the cops doing at the door? What the fuck am I gonna do? Russell looked around the hotel room frantically until he found his shoes.

"One second, I just got out the shower. I need to get dressed right quick."

"Hurry up dude, we just got a few questions," Hampton shot.

Russell reached in the nightstand drawer and grabbed his money and gun. He tucked the gun in his waistline and the money in his pocket before grabbing both of his phones and putting them in his other pocket. He looked over at the window and starred at it for a moment. Well, my uncle always told me be aware of my surroundings, cuz you never know when you gonna have to turn a window into a door.

"Dude, you're making me real nervous out here, what are you doing in there? I need you to open the door now!" Johnson yelled.

"Give me a second, man. I had to dry off first, I'm putting some clothes on now," Russell shot back.

Russell opened the window, but it seemed to only open about five to six inches. "Shit," Russell cursed silently. With all the force he had, Russell pushed the window outward, causing the frame to break and allowing the window to open all the way. Placing both legs out the window, Russell said a silent prayer, asking God not to let him get hurt too bad before shimmying out the window.

"Dude, what the fuck was that?" Johnson asked after hearing the loud noise.

Russell landed on the ground on his knees; when he stood to his feet, he was almost knocked back down again by the pain in his leg. Nevertheless, he knew he had to get the fuck out of there. Limping, he ran as fast as he could around the side of the building.

Johnson placed the key card up to the sensor and pulled down on the knob while Hampton stood in front of the door with his gun drawn. Hampton walked in first with Johnson right behind him. They looked in the closet and bathroom before realizing their suspect had just jumped from the third-floor window.

"Fuck!" Hampton roared.

"He jumped out the window, he has to be still around. Look out for a white Yukon in the parking lot, do not let him leave out." Johnson yelled into his walkie before they both rushed out the room.

"A white Yukon pulled out the parking lot about a minute ago," another officer replied.

Johnson and Hampton ran down the stairs at full speed, in an effort to get to their car as quickly as possible. Johnson could not believe he'd let the man slip right between his fingers. He was so close to catching this asshole, now here he was, back at square one. He could have kicked himself for allowing this to happen.

Once in the lobby, Hampton and Johnson ran to their police car and whipped out the parking lot, in search of the Yukon.

"There he is right there! Pull him over," Hampton yelled out.

Once the Yukon was pulled over, both Johnson and Hampton cautiously approached the SUV with their hands on their guns. They didn't know if he was armed, so they were not taking any chances.

"Can you step out of the vehicle?" Johnson announced as he pounded on the driver's side window.

The man, confused, looked at the officers before opening his door and stepping out of the car. He placed his hands in the air so the officers could see them.

"What seems to be the problem, officers?" Russell asked.

"We had a call about a man at the Courtyard Marriot not too far from here. The man was trafficking underage girls and he also is driving a white Yukon just like this one," Detective Johnson spoke.

"I'm sorry, this has to be some kind of mistake. I'm coming from dropping my daughter off with her mother. I wasn't at any hotel at all," Russell stated.

"Can we see some identification?" Detective Hampton asked.

"I'm only reaching for my ID," Russell stated. Keeping one hand up while placing the other in his pocket.

He pulled out an ID with his face on it, however, the name said James Witherspoon. Detective Johnson matched the name on the ID with the name given by the hotel clerk. This wasn't him and talking to him was wasting time they could have been out finding the monster trafficking young girls.

"It's the wrong guy," Johnson said.

Hampton nodded his head, and they let Russell get away. The two Detective searched for hours and came up empty handed until they finally gave up the search.

Shelby sat at her desk, glad that all the drama had finally calmed down. For the past several hours she had been getting calls about the man who jumped out the window, and she was sick of it. She noticed a man walking up to the desk, and Shelby got up from her seat to great him.

"Hello, how can I help you?"

"Hi, I'm Special Agent Freedman with the FBI. I've been going around to all the hotels in the area looking for a missing fifteen-year-old girl. Have you seen her here?" He asked, pulling out a picture of the girl.

"Oh my God, yes, I have. She was just here maybe two hours ago. Some of my co-workers called Homeland Security because they were convinced, she was being trafficked by the guy she was with," Shelby answered.

"Where is the girl now? She is a runaway and has been reported missing by her mother in Atlanta," Special Agent Freedman asked.

"Atlanta? Oh my God, she's only fifteen. I don't know where she is.

The guy she was with jumped out the window, and the police let the girls go."

"Do you know the name of the Detective that was called?"

"One moment," Shelby replied.

She walked into the back office and retrieved the card to the Homeland Security agent. All the while shaking her head at the fact the child was that young. She could only pray she was found and returned safely to her mother. Shelby walked back to the front and made a copy of the card before handing it to the agent.

"Thank you," the agent said before walking out the door.

Russell's heart pounded in his chest as he pulled up to Travis' apartment. He couldn't believe he'd just had to duck the police twice. He knocked on Travis' door, as he looked around as if the police had followed him there. Once Travis finally opened the door, Russell rushed in, closing it behind him.

"Damn bro, what's wrong?" Travis asked in concern.

"I just had to duck the police twice bro, shit was crazy. I had to jump out the window of the fuckin' hotel. Bro, my leg fucked up right now."

Travis motioned Russell to the couch. Travis had to light a blunt as he listened to Russell tell him what happened.

"Nigga, so the police lookin' for us? Man, I knew I shouldn't have got into this shit with you. Where are the girls?" Travis asked.

"I don't know... once I jumped out the window, I didn't look back. Shit, it was every man for themselves."

Travis couldn't believe this. Russell told him this plan was fool-proof. Now the police were all up in it. A thousand things ran through Travis' head as he rocked back and forth. What if they followed him here? What if the girls talk and start saying names? It's over, we caught. I'm going to jail. Travis pondered.

"Nigga, what you sittin' there all nervous for like you the one just ran from the police?"

"What? Nigga, I am nervous, my name all through that shit. Fuck you mean? Instead of worryin' about why I'm nervous, you need to be callin' those bitches and makin' sure they don't say shit. You also should probably go to the fuckin' hospital 'bout that leg," Travis countered.

Russell shook his head; he knew he wasn't going to no hospitals. If the police were looking for him then the hospital would be the first place they looked. He did, however, pick up his phone and call Hannah. She answered on the second ring, frantically.

"Russell, we been lookin' for you, where are you? Me and Nikki just been out here with nowhere to go. Strawberry and Cream came back and left right out once they seen all the police at the hotel. I don't know what to do. Please tell me what to do, Russell," Hannah pleaded.

"Where are y'all? Did the police try to talk to y'all?"

"Yeah, they tried, but you know we ain't tell them nothing. We at a restaurant down the street from the hotel. All our shit is still in the rooms, the hotel clerks wouldn't let us back in because the room was in your name. What are we supposed to do, Russell... we don't even have no money because it was all in the rooms."

Russell paused for a moment as he thought of a solution. He knew he couldn't be the one to go get them. There was no way he would be caught anywhere near that hotel. He also knew that Travis wasn't gonna agree to go get them either.

"Yo, where is Shamia at?" Russell asked Travis.

"I don't know, probably at home because she not out workin' today. Let me call her," Travis stated. He called Shamia, and handed the phone to Russell.

"Hey Shamia, I need you to do me a favor," Russell spoke. "I need you to go pick up Hannah and Nikki and bring them to me."

"Okay, no problem. Is everything okay?" Shamia asked.

"Some shit went down that I can't talk about over the phone. Imma have them send you their location, and I'll let you know what's up when you get here."

"Okay, no problem. I gotchu," she promised. As she immediately hung up the phone, got dress, and headed to the address that Hannah texted to her.

Shamia pulled up in the parking lot of the restaurant about fifteen minutes later. Both Hannah and Nikki damn near ran to the car, happy to see the familiar face. The restaurant employees were starting to look at them strangely, and they didn't want another run in with the police, so Shamia had pulled up right on time.

"Oh, my God, I am happy to see you," Nikki stated, as she got into the back seat, prompting Shamia to pull off in a hurry, heading to Travis' address.

"What the fuck is going on? Russell called me and told me to come pick y'all up. Said some shit went down, but he couldn't tell me over the phone."

"Yeah, it's all bad," Hannah stated before telling Shamia everything that happened.

Shamia pulled up to Travis' apartment speechless. She never thought what they were doing would lead to the police looking for them. People had sex every day. So what they were doing it for money? In Shamia's eyes, it was doing it for free that should be illegal. She had no clue of the girls being underage, so she truly didn't understand.

Russell was pacing the floor when the three of them walked into the apartment. Shamia could see the worry all over his face, and she felt bad. Nikki walked over to him and began rubbing his back.

"Don't worry, daddy, we will get through this. We just can't stay at that hotel anymore. It worked out better for everyone when we were in an Airbnb anyway. Let's just go back there. We can get right back to the money like we never left," she stated.

Russell smiled at Nikki's efforts to help the situation. In fact, what she was sayin' was true. The Airbnb was much better. There were no eyes on them but theirs, so no one would call the police. Russell nodded his head and pulled out his phone in search for another home to rent. He found one not too far from Travis' apartment. The home was only five bedrooms, but it also had a finished basement so the extra space would make up for the missing bedroom. Russell was able to reserve it, starting the following day, putting his mind at ease.

CHAPTER TEN

Nakia sat in the lobby of her job, as she waited on Raphael to pick her up. Her car had been in the shop for the past three days, and she just wished it would hurry and get fixed. Her car was very old, and she knew she needed another one, but she also knew she couldn't afford it. The five hundred dollars she spent to get it fixed had set her back a great deal, and Nakia would have to work overtime in order to make up for the lost money. Raphael had offered to pay for it, and even though they'd gotten closer over the past couple of months, she'd declined his offer. She did, however, accept his offer to take her to and from work.

"Good afternoon, sweetheart, how was your day at work?" Raphael asked once Nakia got inside the car.

"It was okay, how was your day?"

"It's better now that I see you. Do you want me to take you home to change before we go to Rashaud's game?"

"You don't have to go to his game if you don't want to. You can just drop me off and I can ride with my brother," Nakia replied.

Nakia had introduced Raphael to her children about a month ago, and they instantly clicked. He was the first man she'd brought around her children since their father had passed and she was nervous at first.

However, when she saw how gentle and loving Raphael was toward her children, she knew she'd made the right decision. Nakia had grown strong feelings for Raphael in the short time they'd been dating and even thought she was falling in love. He was so kind and generous that sometimes Nakia had to stop him from doing things for her and her children. Raphael had even gotten close to Jalyn, coming over to Nakia's house to watch football on Sunday afternoons.

"Are you crazy? Rashaud made me promised him I would be at his game, and I'm gonna do just that," Raphael replied.

Nakia smiled at Raphael's response, as they pulled off on the way to Nakia's house. Lexi was out in the front yard playing while Jalyn sat on the porch. Lexi's huge smile greeted them as she ran up to the car.

"Mommy, look... I just learned how to do a cartwheel."

Nakia watched as Lexi flipped in the air twice and landed on her feet with her arms straight up in the air. Nakia smiled and made a mental note to enroll her in gymnastics class.

"Where is Shaud? I just need to go change real quick and then I'll be ready to go."

"He's in his room putting his uniform on. Hey Raphael, what's up, man?" Jalyn said, slapping five with Raphael as he leaned in for a half hug.

"Nothing much, man, just chillin'. Everything good with you?"

"Yeah, I can't call it. Just ready to see nephew whip some ass in football."

Minutes later, everyone was out of the house and headed to Rashaud's game.

The family sat in the bleachers as they watched the game. They screamed and cheered at every touchdown Rashaud made. When the game was over Rashaud's team had won twenty-one to seven, and Raphael took them all out for pizza to celebrate. Nakia loved how they all hung out as one big happy family. Times like that made her miss when the kids' dad was alive, because they would have family time every weekend. Although Raphael wasn't him, his presence filled a void that had been in Nakia's heart for years.

Once back at the house, the four of them walked inside and the kids went to shower and change into their pajamas. Nakia walked into the kitchen and grabbed a bottle of wine and two glasses before walking back into the living room.

"Do you want to watch a movie?" Nakia asked, as she sat next to Raphael on the couch.

"Sure babe, whatever you pick, I'll be happy to watch," Raphael replied.

Russell laid in the bed as he looked at the huge 65" inch television mounted on the wall. He was finally able to breath and not look over his shoulder for the police. There was a light knock at his door before Nikki peeked her head in.

"Do you want some company, daddy?" Nikki whispered.

Russell looked down at Nikki's tight young body. Any other time he would have been happy to give her exactly what she wanted; however, he had already promised his night to Shamia. He couldn't let that pass him up; Shamia was a master at sex and tonight, that's exactly what he needed. He declined, and Nikki exited his room without another word.

Not even ten minutes later, Shamia was walking into the room with Strawberry and Cream right behind her. Russell smiled because he knew with the three of them, it would be a freak session like no other. He lit a blunt then unzipped his pants and exposed his rock-hard manhood.

"Which one of y'all wanna taste this honey bone first?" He asked, as he took a deep pull from the blunt.

"All three of us at the same time," Strawberry replied.

Russell's manhood got even harder with those words. He laid on the bed with his legs spread as Shamia crawled in between them. Both Strawberry and Cream positioned themselves on both sides of him on their hands and knees. The three ladies began licking and kissing all over his shaft. Russell licked his lips before taking another pull from his blunt. He moaned softly, as he enjoyed the feeling. The foursome fucked well into the early morning hours and were all spent once finished.

Russell woke up the next morning to loud screams and glass being broken. He jumped up out of bed and grabbed his robe as he rushed to see what was taking place. He'd just made it into the living room when a glass flew right past his head. If he didn't move to the left, it would have hit him. He watched as Hannah ran at Nikki, raising her foot and kicking her directly in the stomach. Causing Nikki to scream before falling to the floor.

"Hannah, what the fuck?!" Russell yelled.

Before Russell could make another move, Hannah got on top of Nikki, throwing punches like a mad woman. Russell couldn't believe this was going on. In all the years he'd been pimping hoes, this was the first time any of them had gotten into a fight. They were supposed to be a family, with Russell being the glue that held everyone together. However, Hannah was fighting Nikki with pure hate in her eyes. Nikki attempted to shield her face, but Hannah's punches were coming to fast. Nikki screamed for Hannah to stop, but her pleads fell on deaf ears. Finally, Russell walked over to them and pulled Hannah off Nikki, gripping her in his arms.

"Yo man, what the fuck is wrong with y'all bitches? Look at this fucking house," Russell yelled, as he looked around the room.

There was glass all over the floor. The 55" inch television that once set on top of the entertainment center was now laying on the floor with a broken screen. The beautiful center pieces that were once on the end tables were now shattered in thousands of pieces on the floor. Russell became furious as anger shot through his body. The damages that were done to the home would set him back a nice amount of money, not to mention how the owners would definitely not rent to him again. Just when things were going well, leave it to some hoes to fuck it up. Russell thought to himself, shaking his head.

"This bitch thinks she's the shit. That hoe ain't shit and somebody needed to let her know that. I'm the top bitch around this mutha-fucka. Fuck you thought, hoe?" Hannah stated smugly.

"Bitch, it ain't no top bitch! Fuck you thought, is the real question. Look at her fuckin' face. How the fuck can she work like that?" Russell asked.

At the mention of something being wrong with her face, Nikki rushed towards Hannah, cocking her fist back and punching her directly in the eye. Nikki hit her so hard that Hannah's head flew back. If Russell wasn't already holding her, she would have fallen to the ground. Russell, already frustrated, had enough. Letting go of Hannah, he slapped Nikki so hard in the face, that he left his right handprint across her cheek. Nikki screamed out in pain, as she held her cheek. Hannah busted out into laughter, however before she could speak, she was backhanded by the same hand that hit Nikki.

"Y'all hoes think shit is a game? Look at this fuckin' house! Not only is the damage fee coming out of y'all's pockets, but so is the next Airbnb. Because thanks to the dumb shit y'all was on, we not gonna be able to stay here. Simple ass bitches!"

"Russell, it was her. What the fuck was I supposed to do with this wild bitch attacking me like this? If anybody should pay for anything, it should be that bitch!" Nikki yelled.

"Bitch, I know you not talkin' back to me. Last bitch that got outta pocket with me was Tianna, and y'all ain't seen her, now have you? If you don't want to end up like her then I suggest you shut the fuck up," Russell shot back.

With those words both Hannah and Nikki stopped speaking and both thought about the fact they hadn't seen Tianna in months. Fear set in because they could only imagine what Russell had done with her. Not wanting to end up like her, the two girls began cleaning the mess they'd made.

"Bitch, Russell ain't playing with them hoes. You hear him down there yellin' and shit?" Strawberry asked, as she walked into Shamia's room.

"Yeah, I hear them. I guess them hoes got to fighting for whatever reason. I don't know what's up with that shit."

"You know how them young bitches is. They be on that childish shit real bad," Strawberry replied.

"Yeah, they young, but them bitches is still grown. It's no need for them to be acting like that."

"Grown? Girl, them bitches at no fuckin' grown. In real life, I don't even know why they here doing this shit. I heard Nikki wasn't nothing but fifteen and Hannah is seventeen."

"Wait, what? Them hoes underage? That's fuckin' why the police got involved. I had no idea they were that young," Shamia exclaimed.

"Shit, they gotta make money too. They clearly ain't got nobody but Russell, so what the fuck they pose to do?" Strawberry looked at Shamia confused.

"Me and Cream were fifteen when we started this shit too. Only we ain't have nobody like Russell to watch our backs and make sure we were straight. Because of that, we went through way more than we needed to," Strawberry continued.

Shamia didn't know what to say. She had a little sister that was fifteen and she couldn't imagine her being put out on the stroll. Shamia knew all the nasty things those men paid them to do, and girls as young as Nikki and Hannah should not be put in that position. Her heart saddened by the mere thought. She wished there was something she could do to help them get out of the lifestyle; however, she knew the game. Her trying to help them could deem fatal for her, and that was a road Shamia didn't want to go down.

Nikki walked into her room and immediately looked into the mirror. Tears welded up in her eyes as she stared at her reflection. Her left eye had swollen so large that it looked like a black golf ball sitting on her face. Her bottom lip was split down the middle, and the huge handprint that Russell left adorned her cheek. She couldn't believe what had happened. For the first time in Nikki's life, she wished she was at home in Atlanta with her mom and brother.

Nikki lifted the bottom corner of her mattress and pulled out the purple Crown Royal bag she kept there. She pulled out the bills she stashed inside and began counting them. She had just a little over a thousand dollars. Shaking her head at the small amount of money she'd accumulated after months of selling her most prized possession. Russell had promised her a lavish lifestyle, which was a lie. He had also promised her a thousand dollars a week in pay, which turned out to be a lie as well. Everything was a lie, Russell hadn't spoke the truth the entire time she'd been there, and Nikki just couldn't take it anymore. And with that, she decided to leave. She knew a thousand dollars wasn't a lot of money, however, it was enough to get her a bus ticket and an Uber back to her mother's apartment.

With that, Nikki pulled her suitcase from the closet and began throwing items inside. She didn't even know if her mother would welcome her back, and at this point, she didn't care. Anything would be better than this, and Nikki only wished she'd never let this happen. This was her own fault for thinking the grass would ever get greener for her.

"What the fuck are you doing?" Russell's deep baritone startled her, causing Nikki to jump. She looked up to see him standing in the doorway looking directly at her. Damn, how long has he been standing there? Nikki thought.

"Russell, you scared me," Nikki spoke with a nervous chuckle.

"I asked you a fucking question, don't make me ask it again."

"Russell, I-I can't do this anymore. I think it would be best for me if I just went back to Atlanta."

Russell walked inside the room, closing the door behind him. Nikki's heart was pounding harder with each step Russell took towards her. The anger she saw in his eyes made Nikki want to run, but she knew she would never make it to the door. Russell stood in front of her, just looking at her for several seconds before running his hand over her bruised cheek.

"You wanna leave me, baby?" Russell whispered, still caressing Nikki's cheek.

"This just ain't for me Russell. I came out here thinking things would be better than this. I didn't even know that fuckin' was the job, but once I found out, I was told I would be making a thousand dollars a week. That hasn't happened yet. Then on top of that, I'm fighting girls I have to live with. I don't like this Russell, so yes, I'm ready to leave."

With those words, Russell ran his hand from Nikki's cheek to around her neck and squeezed tightly. Nikki's eyes widened when her air supply weakened. Russell placed his free hand behind his back and pulled his gun from his waistline before pacing it to Nikki's temple. Tears ran down her cheeks as she prayed Russell wouldn't pull the trigger.

"I'm gonna tell you this one time, and one time only. You belong to me, ain't no leavin'. The only way out of this for you is death. So, unless you ready to die, bitch, I suggest you get with the program. See Tianna's ass, I sold her and for cheap. But you bitch, I'm not selling, I'm gonna kill you, because I gave yo ass a choice. You said you wanted to be with me, and that's exactly what you gonna do," Russell stated firmly.

Nikki couldn't speak if she wanted to; she could barely breath. Between his gun to her head and his hand around her neck, she knew he was serious when he said he would kill her. Russell didn't shed an ounce of remorse for the fear he was infecting upon Nikki. She wanted to scream for help, but she knew no one in the house would come to her aid. So, she did the only thing she could do, accept her fate.

"So, you stayin' or you dyin', bitch?" Russell asked.

"Stayin'," Nikki said weakly.

Russell removed the gun from her head and placed it back in his waistline before removing his hand from around Nikki's neck and walking out of the room, his point being made. She gasped for air, as tears continued to fall. Nikki was so frightened that she knew then she could never leave him. Although she hated the circumstances, she didn't want to lose her life even more. That night, Nikki cried herself to sleep, praying she would someday find a way out of this mess, alive.

CHAPTER ELEVEN

Nakia followed Raphael into the double doors of the Velvet Rope. She normally wouldn't be caught dead in a strip club. However, Raphael always took her on the dates she wanted, so it was only right she did the same. His father owned the club, and Raphael told her he was next in line to own the club. Nakia figured if they were going to be together then she would have to see it at some point. So, there she was, walking through the dimly lit club filled with ass shaking bitches and dudes throwing money.

Nikki had to admit, the décor was nice. Every couch, chair, and bench were made of red velvet, with all the tables being black marble. The walls were clear and filled with color changing water bubbles which alternated between red, blue, purple, and green. The DJ was playing all the major hits as well, causing Nakia to hit a little two step on the way to their booth.

"This is nice," she spoke loudly, in an effort to be heard over the music.

"If you think is something, wait until you taste the food," Raphael replied.

"Food from a strip club? I don't know how sanitary that is," Nakia chuckled.

"My pops has a dope ass kitchen in this muthafucka, with an even doper chef. Just trust me, babe."

Nakia nodded her head, letting Raphael know she would at least try the food. Within minutes of taking their seats, a waitress walked up to the table to take their order. Raphael placed an order for lamb chops, lobster bites, chicken wings, and truffle fries. Stating that those were all his favorite items on the menu. When the food arrived and Nakia tasted it, she quickly saw why. The food was delicious and should have been featured in a five star restaurant instead of a strip club.

"I'm gonna need some of these lobster bites and lamb chops to go," Nakia joked.

"No problem baby. I'll order you whatever you want to take home with you."

Nakia smiled, knowing she wasn't gonna turn down any food, especially good food. Raphael waved the waitress over to the table and ordered a bottle of Ace of Spades and let her know they would be placing a to go order. Nakia had a good time at the club, drinking, listening to music, and even getting a dance or two from a couple of the girls. Raphael had her all out of her element, and she was enjoying it. They didn't leave the club until well after two in the morning and headed back to Nakia's house for a night cap.

The next morning, Nakia was wakened by soft kisses being placed on her forehead. Smiling, she opened her eyes and looked into the eyes of Raphael.

"Did you sleep good, babe?" Nakia asked.

"I slept next to you, so it was wonderful," Raphael replied.

Nakia stretched before sitting up in bed. "Are you hungry?" She asked. "I can cook us some breakfast."

Raphael nodded his head. "You could do that, or we all could get dressed and go out to breakfast."

Nakia smiled, liking that second option more. She got out of bed to let her children know to get dress, then went back into her bedroom to do the same. Once dressed, Raphael took her and the children to an elegant bistro for breakfast. He loved spending time with them and would do whatever he could to keep a smile on their faces.

"What do you guys want to do when we leave here?" Raphael asked.

"I wanna go to the movies and see The Secret Life of Pets 2," Lexi beamed.

"I wanna go to the arcade and play some games," Rashaud stated.

"And what do you want to do, Nakia?" Raphael asked, looking over at her.

"Oh, I don't know. I'm happy with whatever we do today," she answered.

"Yeah right, we all know you want to go to the mall," Raphael laughed.

Nakia smiled, knowing what he said was true. Raphael pulled his phone from his pocket and searched the movie Lexi wanted to see. There was a showing in thirty minutes at a theater about fifteen minutes away from the bistro. He knew if they paid and left now, they could get tickets and snacks and be seated before the preview.

"Okay, here's the plan. We're gonna go to the movies first, then to the mall. And we will finish our day at the arcade, that way we can eat there, and dinner will be covered. What do y'all think about that?" Raphael asked.

They all agreed, pleased with the set-up of the day's events. Raphael, who didn't have any children of his own, looked at Rashaud and Lexi like they were his own. He was always there for them, never missing a game or a special moment since the day Nakia introduced them. He looked forward to making many more memories with them and hoped that him and Nakia would always be together.

By the time they made it to the arcade, the entire gang was amped up by all the fun they'd had thus far. Raphael paid for gaming cards for all four of them, and since they hadn't had anything since breakfast, they decided to eat before playing. They chatted over burgers and fries before challenging each other in every game the arcade had to offer. For hours they played, having the time of their lives until they become so tired, they could no longer play anymore.

Once back home, both Rashaud and Lexi went up to their rooms and went straight to bed.

"Thank you, Raphael, for being who you are. You are amazing to my kids and that is all I could ever ask for. You make me so happy," Nakia stated.

"I love you and the kids. Making y'all happy is what makes me happy."

Raphael hugged Nakia tightly before leading her upstairs. They took a long hot shower together before crawling into bed, holding each other tight throughout the night.

It was the night before Christmas and Nikki stood in her mirror, looking at yet another black eye. Ever since she'd fought Hannah, Russell had been putting hands on her more frequently. It seemed like every time he thought about that day, he would punch, slap, or kick her, as a reminder that he would kill her if she left. She remembered Christmas with her mother and brother. That was the one time of year that her mother showed she cared. She would always save a few dollars from her Bridge card and make Christmas dinner. She would even steal a few items from various stores and put them under their Christmas tree. It wasn't much, but Nikki missed it just the same. She patted concealer around her eye, in an effort to hide the bruise. She was so into applying her makeup that she didn't realize Shamia had walked into her room.

"I know you sick of that nigga hitting on you. Well at least I am," Shamia stated.

Nikki looked over at her with hurt filled eyes and nodded her head.

"I am, but Russell said he would kill me if I ever left him, and I believe him. He's already put a gun to my head, and I don't want to die," she replied.

Shamia closed the door and sat on Nikki's bed before she responded.

"He can only kill you if he catches you. What if I told you I would leave with you, and we could run away together? It would be much better if we could watch each other's backs."

Nikki looked at Shamia skeptically. She didn't know if Shamia was serious or if this was a set up, so she had to choose her words wisely.

"What you mean?"

"Come on Nikki, I know you must be scared. Hell, I'm scared, and I'm grown. You only fifteen. I promise you, all I'm trying to do is help. I know you want to leave; I figure if someone else leaves with you then you won't be so afraid to go," Shamia stated.

Nikki looked into her eyes and saw she was sincere. She nodded her head and took a seat next to Shamia in the bed.

"How can we leave? Russell not gonna just let us walk out the door. And then, where would we go?"

"Why can't we just walk out the door? I just put this good pussy down on Russell, so his ass is going to be sleeping for at least the next hour. Get yo shit, Imma get mine, and in ten minutes, we gonna walk right out that front door. By the time he wakes up and notices we're gone, we will be far the fuck away from here," Shamia pressed.

Nikki agreed and Shamia told her she would be back in ten minutes. Nikki started throwing things into her suitcase, grabbed her coat and hat, and within ten minutes, Shamia was back in Nikki's room ready to go. With their suitcases in hand, they both made their way to the front door.

"What the fuck y'all doing? Y'all sneakin' around and shit. Where y'all going?" Strawberry's loud mouth yelled.

Nikki turned and faced her with fear-struck eyes, as Shamia placed her finger over her own lips, signaling for Strawberry to stay quiet.

"Bitch, don't be shushin' me, I said what the fuck y'all doing? Ooohhhh... y'all trying to leave, ain't y'all? I'm fuckin' tellin'," she yelled, as she screamed both Russell's and Travis' names at the top of her lungs.

With that, the two of them ran out the house at top speed and jumped into Shamia's car. As soon as she started it, both Russell and Travis ran out the house. Russell and Travis got into Russell's SUV just as the two girls pulled out the driveway.

"I'm gonna kill these bitches, they think they can fuckin' leave me? I made these hoes, ain't neither one of them shit without me!" Russell yelled as he followed Shamia at top speed.

Travis took a deep breath. He truly loved his brother; however, this right here was crazy. He'd gotten in the car with Russell to only try to defuse the situation, however with the anger that was steaming from Russell, Travis didn't think that was possible. All these girls wanted to do was leave, and Russell was indeed going to make that very hard for them. That saddened Travis, but he didn't know what he could do. Russell was his blood, and they were told since childhood to always have each other's backs.

"What are we gonna do?" Nikki screamed, as she looked back at Russell's SUV. It was getting closer to Shamia's car, and Nikki was afraid they would catch them.

"Just hold on, I got this," Shamia replied, keeping her eyes on the road in front of her.

If it wasn't for Strawberry's big mouth, they wouldn't be in the middle of a high-speed chase. Where the fuck were the police when you needed them? Shamia conjured. She turned the corner abruptly, in an effort to lose Russell. However, he was right on her ass no matter what she did. Her heart pounded and her palms dripped sweat, as Shamia gripped the steering wheel tightly. She weaved in and out of traffic, until Russell was several cars behind her. Thinking quick on her feet, she turned into the parking lot of Westland Mall.

"We gotta get out the car," Shamia spoke.

"What? Why the fuck would we do that?" Nikki screamed, confused.

"Listen, we gotta lose these muthafuckas. It's Christmas Eve, and this mall is packed. We can lose them in here," Shamia replied.

She parked in the first space she found, and they both jumped out the car. Running into the mall as they scanned the parking lot in search of Russell's SUV, Nikki spotted him, just as they ran inside.

"Them bitches went inside the mall!" Russell hollered as he pulled into a parking space.

"Look, the best way for us to find them is if we split up. You go in one entrance, and I'll go in another. We know them bitches in there, all we gotta do is find them," he continued.

Travis, not wanting to be a part of any of this, reluctantly agreed. They both walked into the mall from opposite entrances, casing the area in search of Nikki and Shamia. Russell couldn't wait to get his hands on them. He was going to show them firsthand that they were indeed his property. He'd told Nikki the only way she would leave was through death, and apparently, she didn't believe him. His trigger finger itched with every step he took, going in store after store and still coming up empty handed.

Nikki's hands shook as they walked cautiously through the mall, looking over their shoulders every other step. She knew they had to get out of there and get as far away from Russell as they could.

"Don't look back, but Travis is behind us. Just keep walking, and we gonna go out that door right there," Shamia pointed.

Nikki wanted to run to the door, but she didn't want to draw attention to herself, so she kept walking. They were almost to the door when Russell began yelling out to them. With Travis directly behind them and Russell running towards them from the side, they ran at top speed straight ahead and out the door. Running through the parking lot, they didn't stop until they got to Shamia's car and got inside. Shamia pulled out the parking space and turned onto the main road into oncoming traffic.

"I think we lost them... look, it's only one way for us to assure they we gonna be safe. We gonna have to go to the police, Nikki," Shamia stated.

Nikki nodded her head in agreement. She normally would never talk to the police, as a child, she was always told not to tell them anything. However, if it was between dying or speaking with the police, she would take the police for three hundred, Alex. About fifteen minutes later, Shamia was pulling into the Westland Police Department.

"Damn, you got it smelling good as hell in here, sis. You got a nigga hungry as hell," Jalyn stated, walking into the kitchen.

"Well, yo ass gonna have to find you something else to eat cuz this is for tomorrow," Nakia replied.

"Mommy, are we making cookies for Santa?" Lexi asked, as she made her way to the kitchen.

"Yes, we are... matter of fact, you can tell Rashaud to come down here and we can get started now."

Nikki pulled the cookie dough out the fridge and sat it on the counter next to the cookie sheet. After the cookies were done baking, everyone went to take showers and put on their matching Christmas pajamas.

"Is Raphael coming over tonight? I wanna give him my gift tonight," Lexi beamed.

"Yes, he should be here soon. But Christmas is tomorrow, why can't you wait til' then to give him his gift?"

"I'm too excited, I wanna give it to him tonight."

Nakia laughed, she loved how close her children and Raphael had gotten. He was a wonderful man to them, and Nakia couldn't ask anything better. They'd just got into their pajamas and curled up on the couch when Raphael walked through the door.

"Merry Christmas!" Raphael called out, holding up bags filled of wrapped gifts. The children cheered, as Raphael placed each gift under the tree.

"What y'all watchin'?" Raphael asked.

"How the Grinch Stole Christmas... go change into your pajamas so you can watch it with us. Mama got you some pajamas just like ours," Lexi announced.

Raphael smiled and nodded his head. He loved the family dynamic that was being set before him and looked forward to them spending many more years together as a family. From the day he'd laid eyes on Nakia, he knew it was something different about her. She was special. The light she shinned on his life was brighter than anything he'd ever known. Nakia was good to him, and good for him, and he never wanted to be without her. Raphael only knew one way to assure she would be his forever, and that was to marry her, and that's exactly what he planned to do. On Christmas morning after the kids opened all their gifts, Raphael would get on one knee and propose to the love of his life.

"Mama, if I go to sleep, would that make Santa hurry up and bring my gifts?" Raphael heard Lexi ask, as he made his way back to the living room.

"Well, sort of. When you sleep, times seems to go by faster. And since Santa can only come with the kids are sleep, yes, it will seem like he came faster," Nakia replied.

"Okay, I'm sleepy," Lexi closed her eyes and fell out on the couch.

Breathing loudly out of her mouth, causing a snore like noise to ring out. Everyone busted out into laughter as Lexi continued to snore.

"You can't fake sleep, Lexi. It's just like the song says, 'he knows when you sleepin' and he knows when you are awake'," Rashaud spoke.

Lexi continued to lay there with her eye closed, still snoring.

"Lexi!" Rashaud shouted, playfully hitting her on the arm.

"Huh? Oh, I couldn't hear you, I was sleeping," she joked, and everyone laughed even harder. The four of them sat on the couch watching Christmas movies until the children went to sleep.

Lexi was the first one up the next morning. Walking into Nakia's room, she woke her and Raphael first before heading into Rashaud's room to wake him. They all walked down the stairs and sat around the tree. Nakia and Raphael watched as the kids opened gift after gift, showing off everything they opened.

"I have a surprise for you," Nakia stated, picking up a small silver box with a blue ribbon. She handed it to Raphael, smiling from ear to ear.

"Aww baby, you know you didn't have to get me anything. It's my job to spoil y'all," Raphael replied.

"Just open it, baby," Nakia pushed.

Raphael untied the ribbon and opened the box. His face lit up as he looked down at a positive pregnancy test.

"Babe, is this your test? Does this mean we're having a baby?" Raphael asked, shocked but extremely happy in the inside.

"A baby? I'm gonna be a big sister?" Lexi beamed.

"Yes, the test is mine, we are having a baby. And yes, Lexi, you're gonna be a big sister," Nakia answered.

Raphael was ecstatic by the news and knew the decision he'd made to ask her to marry him was the right one. She was carrying his child, so he knew from this day forward, he would never leave her side. Getting down on one knee, he grabbed Nakia's hand.

"Oh my God, Raphael, what are you doing?" Nakia asked, as Raphael pulled a small black velvet box from his pocket.

"Nakia, you are the best thing that has ever happened to me. You have brought these two beautiful children into my life, and now, you're carrying my child. I would be honored if you would become my wife.

Will you marry me, Nakia?" Raphael asked, opening the box and revealing the most beautiful princess cut diamond Nakia had ever seen.

"Oh my God, Oh my God, yes Raphael. A million times, yes!" Nakia cried.

Raphael placed the ring onto her left ring finger, and they hugged each other tightly. Nakia and Raphael were both overjoyed by the next step of their relationship. The children also walked over to them, joining them in their embrace. This was the best Christmas Nakia had in years and it was all thanks to Raphael. She truly couldn't be happier as she admired her ring.

"You know we can't get married until after I have the baby, right? I wanna party like a rock star on my wedding day and having a baby bump will prevent that," Nakia stated.

"I got you, baby; you can pick the date. Just you saying yes made me happy," Raphael replied.

CHAPTER TWELVE

Russell sat on the bed of his Airbnb. It had been months since he'd seen Nikki or Shamia, and the fact that neither one of them were there was hurting his pockets tremendously. He only had Hannah, Strawberry, and Cream, and they just were not raking in as much money as Nikki and Shamia did. Luckily, when he went on to IG to look for another girl, he was able to find one that looked to be a good candidate. She was on her way over for an interview. The pictures she'd posted had Russell drawn to her, and if she fucked anything like she looked, she would make Russell a huge profit. The doorbell rang, and Russell knew exactly who it was. Making his way to the front door, he opened it and greeted the girl on the other side.

"Hello, I'm Tonya, and I'm here to speak with Russell," she stated.

"Hey Tonya, I'm Russell, it's nice to meet you. Why don't you come on in and we can get started."

Tonya walked into the home and looked around, admiring the décor. She knew this man must be getting big money by the way he had his home decked out, and she wanted to get down with his team. She'd never been a prostitute before, however, she loved sex, so if she could make money from it, she was down. Tonya followed Russell to the living room, and they both took a seat on the couch.

"Can I get you something to drink? I got water, pop, liquor, or wine," Russell offered.

"Sure, I'll take a red wine if you have it. If not, water will be perfect."

"One red wine coming right up." Russell walked over to the bar and made the two of them drinks before returning to the couch.

He looked at Tonya's thick thighs and licked his lips before taking a sip from his glass. Russell could tell that Tonya was nervous, and he hoped that the wine would relax her enough for him to do what he wanted.

"Do you smoke?" Russell asked, picking up an already rolled blunt from the ashtray.

"Yeah, go ahead and spark it up."

They sat and smoked while Russell learned more about Tonya. He found out that she was sixteen and lived with her elderly grandmother. Her mother died a few years back, leaving her grandma as the only family she had. The grandma lived on a fixed income and Tonya wanted more out of life. Seeing how she was sixteen, there was no job that would be able to accommodate the lifestyle she desired.

"Why don't we go upstairs so we can get into the second part of your interview," Russell said, standing from his seat.

Tonya nodded and followed Russell through the house. They entered the room, and Russell closed the door behind him. Russell didn't even have to say a word, just watched as Tonya began removing her clothes.

"Come and show me what that mouth do," Russell whispered.

Tonya positioned herself between his legs and began stroking his hardened shaft. Spitting on it before letting in slide down her throat. Russell moaned softly, as he grabbed the back of her head, causing his manhood to go deeper into her mouth. Russell's toes curled as he enjoyed the fellatio. There was a pounding knock on the front door and Russell became irritated by the interruption.

"You wanna go answer that, daddy?" Tonya asked.

"Nah, fuck that. We busy, someone else can get it."

Russell closed his eyes and let Tonya's warm tongue satisfy him. He was just about to climax when someone busted through his door, causing both him and Tonya to jump.

"FBI! Don't move and show me your hands," the man yelled out.

Russell couldn't do anything but shake his head, knowing he'd just been caught. There was nowhere for him to run, and no way out of the situation. He'd been caught red handed with his penis in the mouth of an underage girl.

"Russell Cummings, we have been looking for you for months now," Detective Hampton stated.

Tonya jumped up out of bed and covered her body with the comforter. Detective Hampton looked at her and could see right away that she was young.

"Ma'am, do you have some ID on you?" The Detective asked.

Tonya began to reach for her purse until Russell gave her a look that said, bitch you bet not. Not wanting to get him in any trouble, Tonya told the detectives that she didn't have her identification on her. With that, the officers told her they would have to take her in as a vagrant if she could not provide any identification. Knowing her grandma would not pick her up from jail, she grabbed her purse and handed her ID to the officers.

"Bitch, fuck is you doing?" Russell yelled in frustration.

"Just like I thought, she's underage. This girl right here is only sixteen years old. Pieces of trash like you deserve to go up under the jail," Detective Hampton stated. "Cuff this muthafucka up," he continued.

Russell was brought into the police station with his hands cuffed behind his back. He knew from the moment the police walked into his house that he wouldn't get out of this without doing time, he just didn't know how much. If that bitch would have listened to me, I wouldn't even be here. Simple ass bitch, he thought to himself. Russell was placed in an interrogation room while he waited for the detectives to come question him. He racked his brain trying to come up with a story to explain to the detectives why he was caught with his dick in the mouth of a sixteen-year-old girl. About twenty minutes later, both Detectives Johnson and Hampton entered the room.

"Russell, Russell, Russell, we have been looking for you for damn near a year. Ever since you jumped out the window of the Courtyard Marriott," Detective Johnson stated.

"I don't know what the fuck you talking about. I wasn't at no Courtyard Marriott, and I damn sure didn't jump out no fuckin' window."

"Oh really? Because we have camera footage and witnesses that can place you there with two underage girls. Do you know what the penalty is for trafficking underage girls? It's life in prison, and I'm here to tell you that I'm gonna make sure you get the maximum sentence possible. You're the fucking scum of the earth preying on and selling little children," Detective Johnson shot back.

"I ain't trafficked nobody, fuck is you talkin' bout? Y'all love to try and take a black man down. But y'all got this shit wrong, so I ain't worried about shit. I ain't trafficked nobody, and I don't know shit about nobody being underage. That girl told me she was nineteen, I didn't know until she showed y'all her ID how old she really was. That shit ain't on me if I didn't know."

"You're a fast talker, but I can smell a lie a mile away. And you sir, are fucking lying. It's my job to prove that, and don't worry, I will. I'm great at my job," Detective Johnson assured.

Anastasia stood at the front desk going through all the daily paperwork when the double doors of the hotel opened. A tall white man with dark brown hair walked in and up to the desk. Smiling, Anastasia greeted him.

"Are you checking in?" She asked, still smiling.

"No, I'm not. My name is Special Agent Scott with the FBI. I'm here because last year, a man jumped out of one of the third-floor windows. Were you working here at that time?" He asked.

"Yes, I was here, and I remember exactly what you're talking about. It's not every day that someone jumps out of a window," Anastasia replied.

"Was it you that called the task force?"

"No, it wasn't me. It was my co-workers, Nakia and Bailey. They knew something was going on with that man, and they made the call," Anastasia replied.

"Is either one of them here now?" Special Agent Scott asked.

"No, however, they will be here tomorrow morning at seven."

Special Agent Scott reached into his pocket and pulled out a card and handed it to Anastasia. Letting her know to give both Nakia and Bailey a message to call him in the morning. He had a few questions to ask about the case, and he could only hope they remembered everything that took place. Anastasia agreed to leave them a message and the agent walked back out the door. Anastasia rushed to her phone to let Bailey know what was going on. When Bailey didn't answer, she decided that she would just let them both know in the morning.

Nakia woke up feeling well-rested and ready for the day. Once she was showered and dressed, she headed to the kitchen to make breakfast for her family. Although she was due to be at work in just a little over an hour, she refused to let her children go to school without a hot breakfast. The smell of the food cooking woke Lexi, and she went downstairs to meet her mother.

"Good morning, mommy... good morning, baby," Lexi greeted, rubbing her mother's protruding stomach.

"Mommy, when are we going to find out if it's a boy or a girl?"

"Not until the baby is born. Raphael and I decided that we wanted to be surprised," Nakia answered.

"But mommy, I wanna know soooo bad," Lexi wined.

"And you will, baby, in about four more months. Now go wake your brother and let him know it's time for breakfast."

Lexi skipped out the kitchen and up the stairs as Nakia made their plates. Raphael walked through the door just as they all sat down to eat.

"Good morning family, is everyone ready for this beautiful day?" Raphael asked before kissing Nakia on the top of her head.

"Good morning, Raphael, thank you so much for taking the kids to school for me. I have to leave soon for work, and I don't know where Jalyn is."

"He's with his new girlfriend, I talked to him last night. And I don't know why you're even going to work. I told you months ago to quit your job, babe. You don't have to work at all, especially while you're pregnant," Raphael stated.

"Because I want to work. I have always worked for everything I have. That's not gonna stop now."

"I understand your independence, baby, but I got money over money. It's no reason why my future wife should be working for pennies," he replied.

Nakia smiled because she knew he meant well, however, there was no way she would quit her job and depend on anyone else to take care of her children. She never wanted to be in a predicament to where anything was taken away from her. Although she didn't think Raphael would do anything like that, she didn't want to chance it. So, she kept working.

Nakia pulled into the half empty parking lot at work and smiled, knowing it would be an easy day. She walked into the door cheerfully as she greeted her co-workers. Her smile faded once she walked into the back office and overheard some of Bailey and Anastasia's conversation.

"What do you mean the FBI wants us to contact them?" Nakia asked, confused.

"It's about that guy that jumped out the window last year. They finally have him in custody and they are trying to build a case against him. They just want you guys to contact them and give statements. No big deal," Anastasia announced.

"I told him y'all would be here today, and I would have y'all call him," she continued.

"You told him what? Why would you tell him when we work and you gave him our names? What the fuck, Anastasia? We've already told them what we knew the first time. Why would we even need to give a statement a year later? I don't even remember shit other than he jumped out the window," Nakia exclaimed.

"Exactly, I'm not going to court over this. And when I talk to him, I'm gonna tell him just that," Bailey stated.

"Calm down, it's gonna be fine. He just wants to talk to y'all," Anastasia countered.

Shaking her head, Nakia walked back up to the front. She was pissed that Anastasia gave out any information about her. It was a rule that if anyone came to the desk looking for any employee, they were not to give out any information. Anastasia knew that firsthand, and she had completely gone against the rule. Nakia rubbed her belly, she knew she was not about to call the Detective back. If they didn't get enough information the first time, then that was on them. Nakia had done her job by calling them for the young girls, anything that came after that was up to the Detectives.

By two thirty, Nakia was more than ready to go. She was sitting in a chair at the front desk scrolling through Instagram when a tall dark-haired man walked through the doors.

"Hello, how can I help you?" Nakia asked, standing from her seat.

"Hi, Nakia," the man said, looking down at her name tag. "My name is Special Agent Scott with the FBI. Can I have a few words with you?"

Damn this fuckin' name tag, I should have taken it off the moment Anastasia told me he came in looking for us. She was just about to say yes when Bailey walked up to the front desk. The agent looked down at her name tag and smiled.

"You're just the two that I need to speak with. Can we go somewhere and talk privately?" Agent Scott asked.

Nakia nodded her head and escorted the agent into the back office, with Bailey following behind them. It was at that moment when Nakia pondered quitting her job. If she would have listened to Raphael, she wouldn't be going through this right now.

"I know that you both gave statements to the task force. However, I'm new to the case and wanted to speak with the two of you myself. So, can you please tell me what prompted the two of you to call Homeland in the first place?"

"Yes, we knew he was trafficking those girls, and they looked young," Bailey answered.

"What were some of the things that made you guys think that? Did you see the girls with other men or what was it?" Agent Scott asked, looking directly at Nakia.

Nakia didn't say a word, as Bailey continued to speak.

"The man had two phones, and he was always on both of them

every time I saw him. Then the girls would get in and out of several cars a day. It was pretty much obvious what he was doing to them," she said.

"And what about you, Nakia, did you notice the same thing?"

"I'm not really sure. It was over a year ago. I have a hard time remembering what I saw yesterday. So to remember what happened over a year ago is next to impossible. "

Agent Scott went over a few papers from his clipboard before replying.

"In your initial report, you stated that he told you that he was in a poly relationship with the females he was staying at the hotel with. Do you remember that?"

"Not really, but if that's what I said then okay."

"Well, those were your words. Is there anything else the two of you can tell me?" Agent Scott asked.

Nakia shook her head no, and the agent stood there starring at her for several seconds. It was almost as though he was looking directly through her.

"Let me ask you this, would either of you be able to identify him in a lineup?"

They both shook their heads no and the agent told them that he would be in touch if they had to take it to trial.

"Wait, what do you mean if it goes to trial? I do not want to testify in front of people," Bailey stated firmly.

"Don't worry, I doubt it will even go that far. This case is pretty open shut. He would be a fool to take this to trial," the agent replied.

He handled his card to Nakia before walking out of the hotel. Nakia handed the card over to Bailey because she knew she was never going to use it. She didn't sign up to testify against anything in anyone's court and didn't plan on doing so. Jalyn told her to mind her own business, but she didn't listen. She thought she'd done the right thing for the young girls by getting them away from that predator. However, she was starting to think the best thing for them could have been the worst thing for her.

Russell sat on his cot in deep thought. He needed to get out of jail, and fast. There was no way he could just sit around in there and wait for his trial. He definitely was not taking the plea deal of twenty years they'd offered him, so he knew his lawyer would have to take the case to trial. The judge had given him a half a million-dollar cash bond, so he wouldn't even be able to get a bondsman. With the courts backed up, it could be months, maybe even a year, before he went to trial, and Russell couldn't be a sitting duck.

However, at the same time, he knew he didn't have that kind of money. He hoped that Travis would hold down his business while he was locked up, however, the fear on his face when he came to visit Russell had him second guessing that. Besides, Russell knew that even if his girls worked all day every day, it wouldn't add up to half a million. The only person he knew with that type of money was Fatbar, however, Russell didn't know if he would give him such a large amount. On top of that, if he did, how would Russell be able to pay back the money?

He knew he only had about fifty thousand in his safe and that was before he got a lawyer, not to mention Travis taking from it to keep the Airbnb. There was no telling what was in there now. All he could hope was that Fatbar would have his back and bond him out of jail. The moment he was able to use the phone, he placed the call to Fatbar, praying the entire time the phone rang. Once Fatbar answered, Russell explained to him what was going on the best he could over the tapped jail phone.

"Russell, you know you are like a son to me. So, yeah, I can do that. I would have to kill two birds with one stone though, for this to be possible," Fatbar stated.

Russell held his head low, knowing that was code for he would have to give Fatbar two of his girls in order for him to bond him out. Russell only had three left and didn't want to let anyone go. However, he didn't want to stay in jail more, with those thoughts, he agreed to Fatbar's terms. Letting him know that he would give him Strawberry and Cream. He hated to do it because those two had been nothing but down for him. He knew the evils of the sex trade in Albania and hated to put them through it. Well, at least they will have each other. They can look out for each other. I'm in this muthafucka alone, with nobody to watch my back, so I gotta think about me. Shit, it's kill or be killed. I'll just have Fatbar promise to keep them together. He thought.

Russell hung up the phone after promising to deliver the girls the day he was bonded out. He walked back to his cell smiling, knowing this would be his last night sleeping on this raggedy cot. He laid there, as he thought about how he could still make money while in the midst of a trial. He also needed to get both Nikki and Shamia back with him and away from the access of the police. He knew they were giving statements and would possibly testify against him in trial and there was no way he could let that happen. So, his first order of business once he was free was to find them.

Nakia stood at the front desk, rubbing her belly while she made a reservation for the future guest she was on the phone with. Nakia was hungry and couldn't wait to end the call so she could go warm up her lunch. She'd just finalized the reservation when the last man on earth she wanted to see walked through the doors. It was Special Agent Scott walking over to her smiling.

"Hello Nakia, is Bailey here today? It's something I need to talk to the two of you about, privately."

"Hello Detective, no she's not here today, and I've already told you I don't remember much of anything," Nakia replied.

"Yes, I know what you stated, and if we could talk privately, I'll tell you why I'm here."

Nakia nodded and motioned the agent to the back office. She took a seat in the chair and looked up at Agent Scott as he remained standing. She wanted him to get to whatever it was he was going to say. It didn't matter to Nakia because she was gonna keep the same story and that was, she didn't remember.

"Russell was bonded out this morning and refused to take the plea deal he was offered. Which means his case will go to trial. I just wanted to come here and let you and Bailey know that you may be subpoenaed to testify," Special Agent Scott informed.

Nakia stared at him and blinked her eyes several times as if it would change what he'd just told her.

"Look Agent Scott, as you can see, I'm pregnant. I can't be going to court to testify in a crime. That is unwanted stress that my baby and I don't need to be under. Besides, I have already told you that it was over a year ago, and I don't remember."

"Nakia, we already have your initial statement that we can go over with you before the trial, if you indeed have to testify. You won't be going in there blind; we will prep you first. I understand your concern, but I can assure you have nothing to worry about."

"Oh, you mean the way you assured me he would take the plea huh," Nakia countered. "I'll be sure to tell Bailey everything that's going on, Agent Scott. Thank you for letting me know, and you have yourself a good day."

Nakia stood to her feet, letting Special Agent Scott know that was the end of the conversation. She went into the break room and placed her food in the microwave before pulling out her cell phone to call Bailey and let her know what was going on. She was at her wits end with this situation and didn't know what to do. How did what started off as a normal morning with Nakia clocking into work end up turning into all this?

"I am not fucking testifying! I told him that when he came in the other day. I'm not going in front of nobody's court! Then he's out on bond, like what the fuck?" Bailey yelled into the phone. She was scared as hell because she had no clue what would happen next. What if he came after her? How would she protect herself? They were the same people that let him get away in the first place, so how could they protect her from him? She began to cry out of fear.

"Don't cry Bailey, he said we might not have to testify. They might have enough evidence without us, however if we do, just stick with the story I gave. You don't remember shit."

After calming Bailey down, Nakia ended the call and continued to eat her lunch. When she got off, she went straight home. All she wanted was a hot bubble bath to wash off the stress of the day.

Raphael walked up to the front door of his childhood home and entered. He could smell the food his mother was cooking from the front door, and he couldn't wait to get a plate. He loved his mother's cooking, however, he only had it on holidays or times like now when his father called him over for business meetings. There was no telling what his father needed him to do now, but from the tone in his voice when they spoke, Raphael could tell it was urgent.

"Hey ma, what you in here cooking that's smelling so damn good?" Raphael said, kissing his mother on the top of her head.

Raphael's mother, Harlin, was a beautiful woman, with dark skin as smooth as chocolate. She always wore her hair in a short pixie cut with blonde highlights. His mother and father had been together for over thirty-five years and was more in love than ever.

They were teens in high school when they began dating, in a time when mix relationships were not so common. Fatbar's parents made it known they didn't approve with the relationship. Letting Fatbar know that as long as he was in a relationship with a black woman, he would not be a part of the family. Putting him out the house at the tender age of sixteen. Being out on the streets with nowhere to go gave Fatbar the push he needed to become the hustler he was today.

"Oh, just some oxtail, rice, mac and cheese, cabbage, and cornbread. Nothing too big. When your father told me you were coming over, I knew I had to whip up something. Did you bring Nakia and the kids with you?" Harlin asked smiling.

"No, they're at home. Dad told me he had something to talk to me about, and I didn't want to have them around while we conduct business."

Harlin looked at her son skeptically. "Raphael, do you mean to tell me that you haven't told that girl what you do for a living yet?" Harlin shook her head in disagreement. "How can that woman truly love you for who you are if she doesn't even know?" Harlin continued.

"It's not that easy, ma, and you know that. Telling people what I do will be the fastest way to get me arrested," Raphael replied.

"I'm not telling you to tell people, I'm telling you to tell Nakia. You know, the woman you asked to marry you? The same woman that's carrying your child. If you think she will turn on you, then what the fuck are you doing about to marry her? If you love her Raphael, you have to give her a choice."

"You make it sound so simple. Like really, what am I supposed to say, ma? 'Hey Nakia, how's your day? Oh that's great, mine was good too. I killed three people today and made about a hundred thousand from it.' Like be for real, ma, what woman is just gonna accept her man is a murderer for hire? Especially a woman that's not in the life already?"

"A woman who loves you. I accepted your father and everything that came with him because I love him. A woman that loves you will do the same," Harlin stated.

"That's different, mama, you and pops got into this life together. Y'all had nothing and built this entire empire with y'all own two hands. Nakia comes from a totally different part of the track, and I'm not sure if I'm ready to expose this side of my life to her."

"Well, it's your life. I've said my peace, so you do what you want. Just know if she finds out who you are before you tell her, it's going to be harder on your relationship, and that's something you definitely don't want," Harlin scolded.

Raphael nodded his head and kissed his mother on the cheek. He knew she meant well; however, he knew this was something he would have to tell Nakia on his own time. When he felt the time was right, he would tell her, until then, he would hide it and pray she didn't find out.

Raphael walked through the house until he came to his father's study. He could hear voices and only recognized one as his father's. He wondered who he was talking to, and he opened the door and walked in cautiously.

"Raphael, just the man I've been waiting on. Come on in and have a seat, son," Fatbar said, smiling.

Raphael took a seat, still eyeing the man his father was speaking with.

"Raphael, you remember Russell, don't you?" Fatbar asked.

"No, I don't, but what up doe, Russell?" Raphael reached his hand out for Russell to shake.

"What up doe, Raphael?" Russell replied.

"Well now that Raphael is here, we can get down to business," Fatbar stated.

Russell reached into his pocket, pulled out a wad of money, and placed it on the table in front of him. Before sitting back in his seat and looking over at Raphael.

"What's this?" Raphael asked, pointing to the money.

"Russell here has someone that he needs you to take care of. A couple girls from his organization got away and could possibly take down our organization in the process. He's found out where one of the girls is staying and we need you to take care of her," Fatbar stated.

By mentioning the issue could possibly affect his father's business, he knew he would have to handle it. He picked up the money and started thumbing through the bills. Normally, he would never do a job for a mere fifteen thousand, however, knowing it would help his father, he agreed.

Russell handed Raphael a picture of Shamia, along with an address of where she was staying. Raphael told him he would case the place and would contact his father when the job was done.

CHAPTER THIRTEEN

Nakia laid in bed starring at the wall, she wanted to tell Raphael everything that had been happening at work; however, seeing how she didn't plan on testifying, she decided she would just keep things to herself. She now had three children to think about, and she was not gonna put them in harm's way for anyone. She felt Raphael crawl into bed and wrap his arms around her, pulling her closer to him.

"The baby is growing so big; I wish you would take some time off work now. We don't need the money, so you don't have to keep working. Look, I know you want to work because you enjoy it. However, I think it's putting too much stress on you. You come home every day with your back and feet hurting from standing at that desk, and I don't like that. I'm not saying quit your job, but at least take time off until after the baby is born," Raphael suggested.

"You know what, baby? I think your right. Maybe some time off is just what I need. I mean we haven't even set up the nursery yet," Nakia said.

"I've been setting up the nursery for weeks now," Raphael stated.

Nakia rolled over and looked him in the eyes, confused by what he'd just said. Nakia sat in the small room that she had deemed the nursery every day, thinking of ways to decorate it, so she knew nothing was in there. How has he been working on the nursery for weeks? She wondered.

"What are you talkin' bout, Raphael? There ain't nothing in that room. How have you been decorating it for weeks?" Nakia asked.

Pulling her up from the bed, Raphael told her, "Come on... I can show you better than I can tell you."

"Raphael, you know the kids sleep, we can't just leave them here like that," Nakia objected.

"Come on babe, it will be quick. Besides, they're sleep, so they won't even know we're gone," Raphael countered.

Nakia thought for a moment, as long as it didn't take long, it would be fine. She would be back and in bed before the kids even knew she was gone. With that, she got up and slipped on a pair of sweatpants and a t-shirt before walking out the door with Raphael. About fifteen minutes later, they were pulling up to a gigantic home in the middle of an elegant neighborhood. Raphael pulled into the driveway, got out the car, and went around to the passenger side to open the door for Nakia.

"Raphael, what's this? Whose house is this and why are we here?" Nakia asked, as she got out the car.

The house was beautiful made of cream color bricks with rose bushes all around the front. The grand entrance was made of all glass, and she could see the huge chandelier that hung from the ceiling.

"This is our house, baby, and together, we will make it a home. I told you I want to take care of you and the kids. And my first step in doing that is to give y'all a home to call your own. You will never have to pay another dime of rent again to anyone else, because you are now a homeowner. Everything is in your name, so if anything, ever happens to me, this right here will always belong to you and the children," Raphael stated.

Nakia's eyes filled with tears as she wrapped her arms around Raphael. She never had anyone do anything like this for her or her children, and the joy she felt was overwhelming. Raphael had really come into her life and became her knight in shining armor.

"Thank you so much, baby, I really don't know what to say," Nakia thanked him.

"You don't have to say anything, just come in and look at our new home. I've decorated a few of the rooms because I wanted the house to be fully furnished when you saw it, but I just couldn't keep the surprise from you any longer."

Nakia smiled as they walked into the six-bedroom seven-bathroom home, walking hand in hand. The house was beautiful, with hardwood flooring throughout. Each bedroom had its own bathroom and walk-in closet. However, the master bedroom was breathtaking. The entire ensuite bathroom made Nakia feel like she was sitting inside a rain forest. The shower was made of glass, with a rain showerhead that sat in the middle. There were green potted plants and trees all around the room and double vanity. The jacuzzi tub that sat off to the side of the bathroom looked big enough to fit six, and the lighting in the rooms was awesome. Nakia was in awe as she toured the entire house.

"When can we move in?" Nakia asked cheerfully.

"You can move in whenever you want. This is your house, in your name... so again, if anything was to ever happen to me, this house will remain yours. Nobody can ever take it away from you."

Nakia cried uncontrollably. They got back in the car and drove back to her house.

"Uncle Jalyn is here to save the day!" Jalyn yelled, as he walked into the house.

"Hey Jay, good morning. Damn, I forgot to tell you that I called off work today, so you didn't have to take the kids to school this morning. But, since you're already here, you might as well go head and take them," Nakia laughed.

"Damn sis, everything okay? Is the baby good? Why you call off?" Jalyn asked.

"Yeah, everything is good. I have a surprise for the kids, so I took the day off. I think I'm about to take my maternity leave anyway though. So, I just said fuck work today," Nakia laughed.

"I feel you on that. Raphael been telling me how he's been trying to get you to quit, but you just didn't want to. What made you change your mind, or is that a surprise too?" Jalyn joked.

"I just know some time off will be good for me. I want to spend more time with the kids, plus I gotta get ready for the baby," Nakia replied.

"I feel you on that, you work way too much, sis. So, when can I find out what this big surprise is?"

"Well, if you want to, you can meet me at the kids' school when they get out, and we will head to the surprise."

"Okay, cool. I'll see you then, sis."

Once the kids were off to school, Nakia went up to their rooms and started packing everything up. She was under strict instructions from Raphael not to move anything to the new house herself. He'd already hired movers, and they would be coming to move everything they were taking with them. Two hours later, she'd packed everything in Lexi's room and was now half-way through Rashaud's. Hungry, she walked into the kitchen and made a sandwich before placing a call to Raphael. When he didn't answer, she continued to eat her sandwich before heading back upstairs to finish packing.

Raphael sat in his car in front of the address Russell had given him. The house had been quiet the entire hour he'd been sitting outside, and he started to wonder if anyone was even there. His phone vibrated, alerting him of an incoming call. Looking down and seeing it was Nakia, he let it go to voicemail before putting it on silent. He made sure both his guns were tucked tightly in his waistline before getting out the car and running to the back of the house. Although it was late morning, the neighborhood was quiet, and everyone seemed to be away from their homes.

Using a bobby pin and a metal fingernail file, Raphael picked the lock to the back door and walked inside the house. Pulling out his gun, he walked from room to room. Just as he suspected, no one was home. He walked into the master bedroom of the home, looking through the drawers and the pictures that sat on the nightstand. There was another bedroom filled with a woman's clothing of a different size, which let Raphael know there were at least two women living in the home. He'd just made it back to the master bedroom when someone walked in the house. Raphael quickly hid in the closet so he wouldn't be spotted.

"Girl fuck that. I don't care if that nigga is fine, he gonna have to break bread if he trying to fuck with me," he heard the voice say. When he didn't hear anyone respond, he knew the woman had to be on the phone.

"I know that's right. Okay girl, let me get off this phone so I can hop in the shower. I need to try to catch a lil power nap before I leave back out again."

Raphael watched as the woman undressed. Once he got a clear view of her face, he knew she was the woman Russell sent him for. He heard the water running as she prepared for her shower. Then music began to play. Raphael slowly stepped out the closet, with his gun in hand, ready to shoot. He attached his silencer and slowly crept towards the bathroom door.

Raphael opened the door cautiously and walked in with his gun leading the way. He could hear her singing along to Beyoncé.

He upped his mag and used it to slide the shower curtain back. Before Shamia could even scream, Raphael put two shots in her head, killing her instantly. Within minutes, he walked out the same way he came in, got in his car, and pulled off.

Nakia sat in her car with Jalyn parked behind her as she waited for her children to exit the school building. She couldn't wait to see their faces once she pulled up to the new house and tell the kids it was theirs. She wanted to record it because she knew it would be a memory to cherish. Her phone rung, and she looked down at it, seeing that it was Amanda, one of her co-workers. Nakia declined the call and placed her phone in her purse. Fuck that, she see I'm not at work, so what the fuck is she calling me for?

"Hey, mommy, why are you and Uncle Jalyn here?" Lexi asked as she got into the car.

"Yeah, I was wondering the same thing. Did you forget he was coming to pick us up?" Rashaud questioned.

"No, mommy didn't forget. I have a surprise for y'all, and Uncle Jalyn wanted to see it too."

"A surprise, what is it?" Rashaud asked, looking around the car in an effort to find whatever Nakia was referring to.

"It's not here, we have to drive to it. But we are on our way right now. Buckle up, so we can get going," Nakia said cheerfully.

Nakia pulled off, as the kids began guessing what their surprise was. Lexi came up with the idea that it was a pony. While Rashaud just knew he was about to get a PlayStation 5. Nakia couldn't help but chuckle at the guesses her children were throwing out.

Nakia pulled up to the house and parked in the driveway with Jalyn doing the same. The moving trucks were outside, and the men brought in box after box.

"Mommy, who's house is this?" Lexi asked.

"Yeah ma, who you know with a house this big?" Rashaud asked.

"It is a beautiful home, ain't it? Why don't y'all get out and I'll introduce you guys to the owners."

The children did as they were told and got out the car. Jalyn was already out his car with the biggest Kool-Aid smile Nakia had ever seen. She couldn't help but to bust out laughing as soon as she looked at him.

"Damn sis, who big ass house is this? This shit look like something that would be in Better Homes and Gardens magazine," Jalyn joked.

"Mama said she about to take us to meet the owners of the house," Rashaud answered.

"Hell yeah, I wanna meet them too. I need to find out what they do for a living so I can see how I can get down," Jalyn said.

"You so silly boy, come in y'all," Nakia laughed.

They all walked up the walkway. Seeing how the door was already open because of the movers, the four of them walked right in.

"Sis, I don't think we should just be walking into these people's house like this. This look like the kinda neighborhood where they call the police on black people just for walking down the street." Jalyn stated.

"Boy, shut up. You good, I promise." Nakia laughed.

"Yeah, okay, if you say so."

"You are, silly."

"Don't be alarmed, we're negros," Jalyn yelled out. Reciting Martin Lawrence's line from the movie Bad Boys.

"Boy shut up and come on so I can show you the house," Nakia laughed.

"Umm, I think Uncle Jalyn might be right. I think we should meet the people that live here first before we just start walking through they house," Rashaud warned.

"Okay, I'll give y'all that," Nakia said before turning to look at Jalyn and continuing. "Jalyn, my name is Nakia, this is Rashaud, and that pretty little girl with the two missing top teeth is Lexi. We are the owners of this home. Now can I please give y'all a tour?"

Everyone looked over at Nakia in shock. Lexi was the first one to react, as she jumped up and down, cupping her two small hands over her mouth.

"Mommy, are you for real? This is our new house?" Lexi squealed.

"Nakia, this ain't funny. I done drove all the way over here from the city, who's house is this?" Jalyn asked.

"This ain't no joke, this is our house," Nakia confirmed, holding up the keys and shaking them between her fingers.

"Oh, my goodness, all this is ours, mama, for real?" Rashaud yelled.

"Yes, baby, all this is ours. Now let me give y'all a tour and pick out y'all's rooms," Nakia stated.

They all went from room to room admiring everything. Both Rashaud and Lexi were overjoyed by the amount of space in the new home. Neither one of her children had never seen anything so extravagant in person and now they were living in excellence. Lexi was the first to pick out her room. She loved the window seat in the first bedroom they walked in. Telling Nakia how she could sit in it and play with her dolls.

The nursery was next, and Raphael had decorated it in a safari theme that Nakia absolutely loved. He had lions, elephants, and giraffes hand painted on the walls, with huge potted trees in every corner. The ceiling was the highlight of the room however, with its sky like effects. It went from a funny day with a beautiful blue sky and fluffy white clouds to a peacefully night sky with huge stars.

"Damn sis, this a nice ass nursery. Imma be in here all the time my damn self," Jalyn joked.

"Shit, Imma be right with you," Nakia countered.

Rashaud picked out his room and then Nakia took them outside to show them the best part of the house.

"Oh...My.... God!" Rashaud screamed once he saw the pool and basketball court.

Nakia smiled, knowing her kids were truly happy. It was all about them and their genuine joy that warmed Nakia's heart. She rubbed her stomach and thought about all the happy memories they would make in their new home.

Nikki walked into the house she shared with Shamia, happy to finally be off work. The regular nine to five life was something she had to get used to, and she knew it would take some time. It had been hell for her since she'd let Russell trick her into coming to Detroit, but she was finally starting to feel like she was getting a grip on her own life. Shamia had gone to the police right after they left the mall that day, however, with Nikki being underage, she didn't want to be put in the system. So, Shamia and her both thought it would be a good idea if she stayed in the car while Shamia talked to the police. The constant looking over their shoulders was too much for her because they never knew if Russell would be in the cut somewhere ready to off the both of them.

Nikki had even reached out to her mother. Shamia had told Nikki how the police said her mother had reported her missing, which made Nikki feel bad for having her worry. *Maybe me leaving and her not knowing where I went got her clean. If she's looking for me, that means she wants me to come home,* Nikki was hopeful. However, when Nikki called her, her mother told her that since she left, she was no longer allowed back. When she told Nikki the only reason, she reported her missing was because FIA had threated to cut her benefits off if she didn't, Nikki knew she would never see her mother again. Thankfully, Shamia had done her best to help Nikki out, telling her she would never let her be out in the streets. Shamia rented a small home for her and Nikki to share. Nikki had even gotten a part time job at a local Coney Island, so she was able to help with the bills. Even though Shamia never accepted any of Nikki's money, it felt good for Nikki to be able to offer it.

"Shamia girl, where you at? I need to roll up and tell you the bullshit that happened at work today," Nikki called out, as she walked through the house.

Shamia's car was outside, so Nikki knew she was home. Nikki walked to Shamia's room, thinking that maybe she was sleeping. When she walked in, she heard the shower water running and knew Shamia was in the shower. I'll just go take a shower and roll up. By the time I'm done, she'll be out, and I can tell her about this bullshit. Nikki thought to herself, as she made her way to her room. She went straight to the shower and let the water wash off the stress from her workday.

Once Nikki was done getting herself together, she rolled up a backwood before going back into Shamia's room. When Nikki realized she was still in the shower, she called her name. After Shamia not answering the first time, Nikki called her name louder. When she didn't answer the second time, Nikki walked in the doorway of the bathroom and called her name once more.

Damn, I know this bitch hear me. She ain't fell asleep in no damn shower. Nikki thought, as she slowly pulled the shower curtain back. The sight she saw sent Nikki falling to her knees. There Shamia was, slumped over in the tub with two bullet holes in the side of her head. Blood and brain matter plastered all over the walls and shower liner, as blood ran down the drain. It was clear to Nikki that Shamia was dead.

Nikki's entire body shook, as she threw up in the toilet. The sight of blood was something she could never stand. She knew nobody else had done this other than Russell. If he'd successfully unalive Shamia, Nikki knew she was his next target. So, after cleaning up her mess, she brushed her teeth and began packing up clothes. She grabbed her money from her nightstand before calling the police, reporting Shamia's murder and describing Russell as the suspect. Once she'd left her anonymous tip to the police, Nikki left the house, not knowing where she would go from there.

"What should we have for dinner in the first night at our new house?" Raphael asked.

The movers had just finished placing every piece of furniture in their designated areas, and it was now just the four of them together. Raphael could see that his new family was happy, and that was all he could ask for. Him being able to make them content made all the secrets he'd kept worth it. It was also times like this that made him think he didn't have to tell her. What she didn't know could never hurt her, and the last thing Raphael wanted was for Nakia to be hurt on his behalf. So, for now, he would keep what he did for a living to himself.

"What about tacos?" Rashaud suggested.

"I can do Mexican," Nakia agreed.

Lexi nodded her head, letting everyone else know she was cool with tacos as well. Raphael wasted no time getting on the Uber Eats app and ordering Armando's. Nakia grabbed her phone and began replying to all the missed texted messages she had. It had been hours since she'd looked at her phone, and she had so many. Simone had texted her several times asking if the kids could come over this weekend. She said she would have her niece and nephew and wanted Rashaud and Lexi to come over. Nakia immediately texted back, letting her know she could pick them up Friday evening. The next text Nakia answered was from Amanda. Nakia called her after she'd sent a text telling Nakia it was urgent that she speak with her.

"Hey girl, what up doe?" Nakia greeted.

"Girl, I've been trying to call you for hours to tell you this shit," Amanda presumed.

"My bad girl, what's the tea?" Nakia asked, as she walked out the kitchen. Nakia could tell Amanda had some juicy work gossip, and she couldn't wait to hear it.

"Girl, this guy came in here today. Said his name was Special Agent Scott. He left paperwork for you and Bailey saying y'all have to testify in court and everything. He said if y'all don't cooperate then he will put a warrant out for y'all for obstruction of justice," Amanda spoke.

Just like that, all of Nakia's happiness was down the drain, and she felt as if she could no longer function. She had to take a seat on the couch so she could attempt to get herself together. She rubbed her stomach as she thought about her own children. She couldn't be away from them, so a warrant out for her arrest was most definitely out of the question.

"What do you mean? I told that man I didn't remember anything?" Nakia stated, trying to sound as calm as possible.

"I don't know girl, but if I were you, I would call him. He sounds serious," Amanda spoke.

"Okay girl, thanks for letting me know," Nakia uttered before ending the call.

Nakia sat on the couch rocking back and forth. Everything that agent had told her was a lie. First, he said the case would never go to trial because the guy would take the plea deal. Then he said they wouldn't have to testify because they had more than enough evidence for a conviction. Now this muthafucka was taking paperwork to Nakia's job, forcing her to indeed testify. Not knowing any other way out of this, Nakia decided she would call the agent in the morning.

"You okay, babe? You look like you just seen a ghost," Raphael stated, as he walked into the living room.

"Huh? Um yeah. Wait... what you say?" Nakia jumped, startled by Raphael's voice.

"I asked if you were okay," he repeated.

"Yes, I'm fine, baby. I'm just taking all this in. This is a huge house, and I still can't believe it's mine," Nakia lied. She didn't want to tell Raphael what was going on because she didn't want to get him involved. Besides, even if she did tell him, it wasn't anything he could do about the situation. So, Nakia chose to keep it to herself.

After the family ate their dinner, the children went to bed. Nakia headed up to her room to take her first shower in her new bathroom. The shower was so relaxing, she'd almost forgotten about the bad news she'd gotten just moments before. That was until she got out and it all came back to her. She laid in bed, cuddled next to Raphael as thoughts of possibly being forced to testify in court played in her mind.

When Nakia got to work the next morning, Bailey was already sitting at her desk waiting on her to arrive. Nakia could see the fear in

Bailey's eyes as soon as she looked up at her. Without a word, Bailey handed Nakia the paperwork the agent left for them, and she began to read over it.

"This is some bullshit, then it's not even in an envelope, and he just leaves them here at our job for everyone to see? Is this shit even legal?" Nakia asked, clearly irritated.

"We need to call him right now, girl, because I don't like this shit at all," Bailey commented. Grabbing her purse, Bailey pulled out the card the agent had given her and dialed his number, placing the call on speaker so her and Nakia both could speak with him.

"This is Special Agent Scott," he greeted.

"Hello Detective, this is Bailey and Nakia from the Courtyard Marriott. We have received the papers that you just left up here for us, and we have some questions for you," Bailey spoke.

"Yes, hello, I'm glad the two of you called me back. I would be happy to answer any questions you may have."

"Well, what happened to us not having to testify? You told us you guys had more than enough evidence for a conviction, so why are we being forced to testify?" Nakia asked.

"Yes, I know I said that... however, things changed. The star witness we had is no longer with us. So unfortunately, we need the two of you to testify."

"Wait, what do you mean she's no longer with you? Like she said she wasn't gonna testify?" Bailey asked.

There was a long pause before the agent began to speak again.

"Well, I probably shouldn't be telling you this, however, I want to give you two the truth. The witness was found murdered in her home the other day."

"Murdered? Hold up, what do you mean she was murdered? So, they got to her and now you want to put us in harm's way by forcing us to testify? You can't be serious," Nakia asserted.

"Well, that is not true. As far as we know, her murder has nothing to do with the trial. Russell has been on tether since he was bonded out. We've already tracked it, and he was nowhere near the area when the murder occurred," Special Agent Scott answered.

Nakia and Bailey looked at each other skeptically, and Nakia shook her head no. There was no way she was testifying in shit. They clearly couldn't keep anyone safe if their star witness was murdered on their watch. So, Nakia was in no rush to be in anyone's court room.

"Fuck that, I'm not doing it," Bailey mouthed.

"You telling us your star witness was murdered makes us hesitant to testify. As you already know, I'm pregnant and I have two other children to look out for. I'm not losing my life for anyone. You're just going to have to find someone else to testify," Nakia stated firmly.

"That's not how this works. The two of you have already been subpoenaed by the courts, so you no longer have a choice in the matter. Both of your names have been placed in documents and everything. At this point, if you don't testify then you will be arrested," Special Agent Scott informed.

"Well, let me ask you this, is there a witness protection program for us to enter? You literally just told us the witness you were counting on was murdered in her own home, and you just expect us to freely put our own lives at risk for you? That makes no sense," Bailey commented.

"Well, I also told you that her murder had nothing to do with the case."

"How does that even make sense? We both know he had her murdered. If he didn't do it himself, he had someone else to do it. Either way, he is responsible for it happening," Nakia countered before getting up and walking away. She was tired of the entire conversation and had nothing else to say.

CHAPTER FOURTEEN

Russell walked into his lawyer's office, happy to find out the names of the new witnesses the prosecution had. His lawyer was gonna make sure he did the job he was paid to do, and that was to keep Russell out of prison. There was no way any of the witnesses would make it to testify against him at trial, because Russell was going to make sure none of them lived to say a word.

"Good morning, Kyree, talk to me nice," Russell stated, walking into his lawyer's office and taking a seat.

"Hi Russell, good morning. Now listen, I know you are here for the names of the witnesses, and I'm going to give them to you. I just need you to promise me something first," Kyree said.

"And what's that?"

"You have to promise me that you make it look like an accident. Although they don't suspect you in Shamia's murder, they will start to if every witness for your trial gets murdered," Kyree stated.

Russell nodded his head in agreement because he knew his lawyer was right. Although he was keeping his hands clean by not actually doing the killing himself, he was still paying people to do them. He didn't want anything to come back on him.

"I got you; I'll have them set it up right," Russell assured.

"Okay, I'm trusting you. I don't want to get disbarred for evidence tampering, but at the same time, winning this case would be a good look for my career. So, Imma do whatever I have to do to make sure we win the case," Kyree stated.

"I got you."

Kyree handed Russell a piece of paper with two names on them and told him those were the two hotel workers that were to testify against him. Russell handed Kyree five thousand dollars and thanked him for the information before walking out the office, feeling like he was on top of the world. He knew that once he took care of the two names on the list and found Nikki, he would get off scot-free.

Russell got into his car and placed a call to Fatbar. He'd told Russell that if he could get the names of all the witnesses, that Fatbar would have them taken care of, so he wanted to give him names as soon as possible. Fatbar told him to come to the house and not to speak at all over the phone. Russell agreed and told him he would be there within the next twenty minutes.

Nikki walked inside a Coney Island, stomach in knots from the mess that she called a life. All she wanted was a hot shower and bed to sleep in, however, she didn't know where either of those would come from. There was no way she would be able to go back to the house she shared with Shamia. It was now a crime scene, and on top of that, Russell knew exactly where that was. With her only being sixteen, she couldn't even rent a hotel room. Nikki had been out on the street for days and it was becoming exhausting.

She sat a booth in the back of the restaurant and looked over the menu. She was just getting ready to call the waitress over to place her order when a familiar face walked up to her and sat down across from her.

"Damn sexy, I thought that was you. Long time no see. You out here alone or you not working?" The middle-aged man asked.

The man used to be one of Nikki's regulars when she worked with Russell, and each time he paid for sex, he would only want her. Nikki smiled back at the man, happy to see him, because she knew she would be able to use this to her advantage.

"I'm not working, I don't work with Russell anymore," she answered.

"Yeah, I don't think Russell even works anymore. Every time I try to go on the website, it's been shut down. Do you know what happened?" He asked.

"Nah, I don't. I stopped working with Russell a minute ago," Nikki answered, not wanting to give out too much information.

"You ordering something to eat? The least I can do is buy it for you," he offered.

Nikki smiled, knowing she had him right where she wanted him. This would be her way to at least get a room for a few days, hell, she could probably get him to pay for it too. He called the waitress over to the table and they placed their orders. Once they finished eating, he told Nikki how he would love to get something going like old times. Nikki smiled and let him know if he got her a room for a few days, she would put it on him so good, he wouldn't want to leave. The john agreed and the two left the restaurant together.

Nakia pulled up to McDonald's and placed her order. She knew after the day she had at work, she would not be cooking anything. She'd also made up in her mind that she would put in her two weeks' notice the following morning. She'd gotten tired of the hardships of the job and just going to work could potentially cost her her life. There was no way she was gonna let her children live in a world without her in it, so she was gonna do whatever she had to do to make sure that didn't happen.

"Hey, mommy, how was work?" Lexi asked, as soon as Nakia walked in the house.

"It was good, baby. I brought McDonald's home for dinner. Go get your brother so we can eat," Nakia replied.

The three of them sat at the table, eating their meal and talking about their day.

"Are y'all ready to go over Auntie Simone's house tomorrow? I heard she has a fun weekend planned for y'all," Nakia spoke.

"Yeah, we haven't went over there in a long time. She always takes us shopping every time we go to her house and buys us whatever we want," Lexi confirmed.

Nakia chuckled, knowing how much both of her children loved shopping. She also was excited they would be gone for the weekend. Although Nakia loved her children to life, she also knew she needed some self-care time. She'd been under a lot of stress that she had been keeping to herself, not even Raphael knew what was really going on. Nakia vowed to unplug for the weekend and spend her time getting herself together. She also vowed to herself that tomorrow would be her last day at work. Fuck putting in a two weeks' notice, her mental and physical health were at risk, and that's what she had to focus on.

Nakia called Raphael once the children went to take their showers. She hadn't talked to him all day and wanted to know when he'd be home. She knew that having him around would calm her down tremendously. His vibes were always positive and that was something Nakia loved about him. His ability to make her happy in her darkest moments was something Nakia craved.

"Hey, beautiful, I was just thinking about you. How was your day?" Raphael greeted.

"It's better now that I'm talking to you. What you doing? What time will you be home?"

"I'm on my way to see my pops. We got some business to take care of at the club, then I'll be home after that. You good, baby?"

"Yeah, I'm okay. I just want to cuddle with you," Nakia spoke.

Raphael smiled, loving the fact that Nakia loved being under him. Raphael promised Nakia he would be home as soon as he finished everything with his dad. Nakia ended the call and went upstairs to run herself a bubble bath.

Raphael walked into his father's office, greeting him with a hug. Fatbar poured two glasses of bourbon and handed one to Raphael before they both took seats on the couch.

"So, what's up, pops? You got something for me?" Raphael asked.

"Well, Russell came over today and brought me the names of two more witnesses. Niko volunteered to take on one of the jobs, so I gave it to him. This is yours," Fatbar said, handing Raphael an envelope with money, a name, and a picture of the woman inside.

Raphael studied the picture of the older white woman. Her name was Bailey McDonald and to Raphael, she looked like the type to testify against someone in court. He took a sip from his glass, as he read the address that was written on a sheet of paper. He nodded his head and let Fatbar know he would get it handled his weekend.

"Good... that's the same thing Niko said. The faster y'all get this shit done, the faster we can get the fuck outta this. I like to keep my hands clean when it comes to shit like this," Fatbar stated.

"Your hands are clean in this shit, pops... you don't even know the names of the people. Only one that knows is me, and now Niko. You know we both skilled in this shit so everything gonna be good. Niko got this, and so do I," Raphael assured.

"Yeah, I know y'all got this. If it's anyone I trust to handle business for me, it's you and your cousin Niko. I know I can't go wrong with y'all."

"Yeah, you know we got you, pops," Raphael said, as he drunk the rest of the liquor in his glass.

"Did mama cook anything? My stomach feelin' a bit empty," Raphael continued.

"Yeah, you know once she found out you were coming over, she cooked. Hell, she probably made your plate too," Fatbar joked.

Raphael nodded his head, happy to hear that he'd be eating some of his mama's good home cooking. He hugged his dad before walking out his office and heading to the kitchen. Just as Fatbar said, Harlin had made his plate and put it inside the microwave.

"Hey son, how you doing today?" Harlin asked, as she walked into the kitchen.

"I'm good, even better now that I'm bout to eat some of your food. You know I love your meatloaf. How bout you, you doing okay, mama?"

"You know me, I'm good when my family is good. How is Nakia and the kids?"

"They're good, just waiting on our new little buddle of joy to arrive.

You know we moved in together. When you and pops gonna come by and see the new house?" Raphael asked.

"I'm so proud of you, son, I can't wait to come see it. Why don't we get together sometime next week for dinner? Just see what day works best for you and Nakia and your father and I will be there," Harlin answered.

"Okay great, I'll talk it over with her and let y'all know."

"Sounds good to me. Now while we on the subject, did you tell Nakia yet?" Harlin asked.

Raphael looked at his mother and shook his head. She knew this was the last thing he wanted to talk about, seeing how he'd already told her how he felt about the situation.

"No, I haven't. I don't know when I'm going to tell her, ma, but I know it's not going to be while she's pregnant. That would be a lot for anyone to handle, let alone a pregnant woman. I don't want to add any unnecessary stress to our unborn child," Raphael stated.

Harlin nodded her head, understanding exactly where her son was coming from. Stress could cause so much harm to the baby Nakia was carrying. Harlin wouldn't forgive herself if Raphael told Nakia the truth on account of her, and then Nakia went into premature labor. So, she decided she would back off and let Raphael handle his own business.

Harlin sat and talked to Raphael as he ate, then walked him to the door when he was done. She kissed her son goodbye and watched as he got inside his car and pulled out of the driveway.

Russell laid in his bed watching TV, smiling at the fact he was about to beat the system. They thought they would throw him under the jail, but Russell had pulled their card. He knew in just a few short days, every witness the prosecution had would no longer be breathing. Without the witnesses, there was no evidence against him. No evidence meant no case, ultimately meaning that Russell would be a free man. Russell grabbed the blunt from his ashtray. Fuck the court, he was going to get high and celebrate his accomplishment. He took a deep pull from the blunt and allowed the smoke to invade his lungs. The cocky attitude he bestowed made him feel untouchable. He couldn't wait to see the prosecutor's face once he realized all of his witnesses were not coming to testify. He smiled at the daydream of the judge pounding his gavel saying, "case dismissed."

A knock on his door broke him from his thoughts as he yelled to the person to come in. Travis walked in, holding his head low. If Russell didn't know any better, he would have thought his brother had been crying.

"Bro, you good? What's wrong with you?" Russell asked, confused. He'd never seen his brother this way and needed to know what was going on.

"I just got a call from my homeboy in the hood. He told me Shamia was found murdered in her home a few weeks ago. That shit fucked me up cuz Shamia was good people. I don't understand why anybody would wanna off her," Travis informed him, hurt evident in his tone.

Russell looked at his brother confused. I know this nigga not over here hurt about some snitchin' ass bitch. Fuck did he think would happen to her? Russell swung his feet over the bed, sitting straight up and taking another pull from the blunt before he responded.

"Yeah, I heard 'bout that, and if you ask me, bitch got what she deserved."

"You heard bout it? Fuck that mean? Did you do dat shit, Russ?" Travis asked, scrunching up his face as he starred at Russell, waiting on an answer.

"Did I what, kill her? Nah, I ain't kill nobody. I said, I fuckin' heard about it' is what I said," Russell stood from the bed and walked over to his brother, looking at him up and down, waiting for him to respond.

"How would you hear about it? Yo ass don't watch no fuckin' news. You didn't even know her until I introduced you, so how would you hear about it?"

"The bitch a snitch. She the reason I'm in the situation I'm in now. Fuckin' difference does it make how I heard about it? The bitch is dead, fuck her!" Russell spat.

Travis looked into Russell's eyes, trying to figure out what made his brother so cold-hearted. Shamia didn't deserve to be murdered in her home and at such a young age. She didn't even get a chance at life, and by his brother's nonchalant attitude, Travis knew he had something to do with it. Travis let Russell talk him into becoming a part of his trafficking scheme, but what he wouldn't do was become accessory to murder after the fact. Especially the murder of a woman.

"No, you're the reason you in the situation you in. Nobody told you to start pimping out young ass girls. It's hella grown ass bitches that would do that shit, but you chose kids. That was your mistake. Now you adding murder to the list? Nah bro, I ain't with that shit," Travis stated firmly.

Russell chuckled and walked up on his brother. He was so close to his face; Travis could feel his hot breath from the backwood he was smoking.

"Look nigga, if you ain't for me, you against me. All those against me end up in a grave next to Shamia's. Brother or no brother, a snitch is a fuckin' snitch. You choose right now what you going to be."

Travis nodded his head in understanding, not wanna any smoke with Russell. Travis knew the anger he was feeling might cause him to do something he will regret later. So, instead of keeping the conversation going, he walked out the room, closing the door behind him.

Russell's blood boiled, as anger shot through his body. He hoped his brother wasn't trying to turn on him. He would hate to have to off his brother, however, Russell knew he would have anyone that tried to get him locked up handled. So, if Travis wanted to go that route, he would be sealing his own fate. With that, Russell was content with whatever decision he made.

CHAPTER FIFTEEN

Nakia stood over the stove, scrambling eggs as she rapped along to Cardi B's verse on the Migos Type Shit. She'd woke up that morning feeling wonderful and even decided to go in to work that morning, to work one last shift with her friends. Although Nakia hated the job, she loved the majority of her co-workers, and she at least wanted to say her goodbyes. After today, she would no longer be an employee of the Courtyard Marriott, and that alone made Nakia happy.

"Damn babe, you didn't have to make breakfast. I was just coming down here to do it." Raphael voiced.

"It's okay, babe, I got it. I'm in a great mood this morning, I wanted to cook," Nakia stated.

"That what's up, boo. I'm happy when we're happy," Raphael replied.

"What you got up for the day?" He continued.

"Well, I'm gonna go to work today to tell everyone I'm leaving from my own mouth. Then after I pick the kids up from school, I'm gonna get them ready for Simone to pick them up for the weekend. What about you?" Nakia asked.

"I'm free this morning, so I'll just be hangin' around the house.

Later tonight though, I have some shit I gotta handle with my pops. So, I'll pick the kids up from school today," Raphael answered.

Nakia walked up to him, hugging him tightly. "Let's have a date night tomorrow. We can go out to eat, go catch a movie. It will be fun for just the two of us to be out without the kids for a change," Nakia suggested.

"Yeah, babe, we can do that, whatever you want. I also forgot to tell you that my mama and pops want to come over sometime next week to have dinner with us and see the house."

"Yeah, they definitely need to come," Nakia agreed.

Nakia finished cooking while Raphael went to get the kids up for school. Nakia made everyone's plates and sat them on the table, so they could have a nice family breakfast. Raphael even washed the dishes when they were all finished, and Nakia drove the children to school before heading to work.

Nakia pulled up to work and parked her car. She sat in her car for several minutes just looking at the building. The hotel had left her with so many memories, both good and bad. She'd also made a few friends that she knew she would have for the rest of her life, and she was very thankful for that. Nakia walked into the hotel and went into the back to clock in.

"Hey girl, how you doing this morning?" Bailey asked, as she sipped from her cup of coffee.

"I'm wonderful, today is my last day," she replied.

Bailey sat her cup of coffee on her desk and looked up at Nakia. "Today's your last day doing what?"

"It's my last day working here. I decided to be a stay-at-home mom. My fiancé makes enough money to where I don't have to work... I only did it," Nakia informed.

"That's what I'm talking about. You deserve this, Nakia. I've watched you go through so much, and I'm happy to finally see you happy," Bailey replied, standing up and giving Nakia a big hug.

"What's going on in here?" Anastasia asked, as she walked inside the office.

"Today is Nakia's last day here," Bailey announced.

"Wait, what? Your quitting? Why?" Anastasia asked.

"It's just time for the next chapter in my life, and this place is not included in that. I mean it's not like y'all never gonna talk to me again, my number will still be the same. We will definitely keep in touch," Nakia stated.

"We have to get lunch and put together a little goodbye party. Did you tell Shelby already?" Bailey asked.

"No, I'm gonna tell her when she comes in today," Nakia stated.

Bailey grabbed the stack of restaurant menus from the cabinet and handed them to Nakia. She told her to pick whatever she wanted, and Bailey would buy her a farewell lunch. Nakia was always down to eat so she began flipping through the menus before settling on Chinese.

Her workday went by smooth, and it was bittersweet when she went and clocked out for the last time. She hugged everyone, and they all rubbed her stomach one last time before she walked out the door. Knowing she wouldn't have to pick up anything for dinner tonight, seeing how the kids were going to Simone's house for the weekend, she went straight home. The kids were already home and packing their clothes when Nakia got there.

"Hey, mommy, hey, baby," Lexi greeted, running up to Nakia and wrapping her arms around Nakia's stomach.

"Hey, baby, are you almost ready to go over Auntie Simone's house?" Nakia asked.

"Yep, I'm almost ready. I just gotta pack my baby dolls, some clothes, and I'll be ready to go."

"Okay, baby, you do that. I'm gonna go and see if Rashaud is ready," Nakia said. Rashaud was sitting on his bed playing his game when Nakia walked in his room. Before she could ask, Rashaud told her that all his stuff was packed, and he would be ready when she was. Nodding her head, she walked out of his room and went to her own. She placed a call to Simone, and she informed Nakia that her niece and nephew were ready for her to pick them up.

"Yeah, about that, can you bring them to me? My sister brought my niece and nephew over already, and it won't be enough space in my car for everyone."

"Yeah, that's cool, I'll be leaving here in about fifteen minutes," Nakia stated.

Hanging up the phone, Nakia pulled off her work uniform and changed into something more comfortable.

"Hey babe, how was your last day of work?" Raphael asked, as he walked into their bedroom.

"It was good, they brought me lunch and everything. It was actually a really good day," Nakia informed.

"That's good to hear, babe. Are you getting ready to take the kids to Simone's house?"

"Yeah, we gonna be leaving here in a few minutes, what time you leaving?" Nakia asked.

"Probably not for another hour or so, I wanna give my dad time to get to the club."

"What time you think you gonna be back home? I can pick up some takeout if you want and we can watch a movie or something?" Nakia suggested.

"Yeah, whatever you pick up will be good with me. I shouldn't be home too late; it should only take a few hours for us to get done. Then I'll be right back here, spending time with my favorite girl," Raphael smiled.

He walked up to Nakia and kissed her on the top of her forehead before hugging her tightly. Nakia melted into his strong arms as she inhaled his cologne. She couldn't wait to spend the weekend together, just the two of them. It wasn't often they did anything without the kids, so Nakia was about to enjoy every minute of this.

"Mommy, I'm ready," Lexi said, walking into the room.

"Okay baby, go get Rashaud and tell him we're ready to go," Nakia replied.

"Let me go so I can get back. The quicker we both get back, the quicker we can start our weekend."

"I can't wait, I'll try to make this quick, so I can be back as soon as I can," Raphael replied before kissing Nakia goodbye.

Nakia and the kids all got in her car and headed to Simone's house. When they pulled up, Simone was sitting on the front porch sipping on a glass of iced tea, as she watched Evan and Talia play in the front yard. Lexi was the first to get out the car, running up to Talia, letting her know about all the dolls she'd brought for them.

Rashaud, who wanted to play it cool, got out the car with his backpack over one shoulder while holding a PlayStation controller in his hand.

"Hey bro, I see you brought your PlayStation, what games you got on there?" Evan asked.

"I got a lot, let's go hook it up and pick something to play," Rashaud responded.

"Hey girl, look at the stomach on you. I can't wait for you to drop so I can spoil my new niece or nephew. Hell, are you sure you're not having twins?" Simone joked.

"Bitch shut up, it's only one baby in here. If it did end up being twins, one of them would be living with you," Nakia laughed.

The two friends embraced, and Simone poured Nakia a glass of sweet tea from the pitcher that sat on the table beside her. The two sat down and began to catch up on what had been going on in their lives the last few weeks. Nakia, finally ready to get her secret off her chest, told Simone about the case the state was trying to get her to testify in. It felt like a weight was lifted off of her shoulders. Simone looked at Nakia in shock with her mouth hung open.

"Girl, why you ain't tell me you was going through all that? You know I would have been here for you," Simone tried to console her.

"I didn't tell nobody, not even Raphael knows. I've just been keeping it to myself. Getting into someone else's business is how I got into this situation in the first place. I didn't want to do that to anyone else."

"So, what you gonna do? You gonna testify in the trial? I know you gotta be scared, cuz I would be."

"Bitch I'm scared as fuck, I don't want no parts of this shit. The agent telling me if I don't testify, I can go to jail. Girl, I can't go to nobody's jail. So, I really don't know what I'm gonna do. I just wish this shit would go away," Nakia voiced. Nakia took several sips from her sweet tea before continuing to speak. "I should have just minded my own damn business like Jalyn told me to."

"Damn friend, everything has to work out. You can't be testifying while you're pregnant. What if you go into labor while you're in court? This is too much. Imma have to turn this sweet tea into long island fuckin' with you," Simone said before standing up and walking into the house. Returning minutes later with a spiked drink.

The two friends talked for a couple hours, as they watched the girls play outside. Once Nakia got hungry, she decided it was time for her to go. Simone told her that she would drop the kids off to her Sunday evening after her sister picked up Evan and Talia, and Nakia got in her car and left. Deciding on Indian for dinner, she made a stop to pick up the food before heading home.

Bailey pulled into the Kroger's parking lot and got out her car. She hated going to the grocery store so late, however, she'd just gotten off work and had nothing at home to cook for dinner. She decided she would just do her shopping for the week while she was already at the store. Making her way through the aisles, she picked up everything she knew she needed, plus some of the things she didn't. Bailey hated going to the grocery store hungry, because she always spent more money than she wanted to, but tonight, she didn't have a choice. After paying for her items, she went to her car, eager to get home and cook her delicious meal.

She pulled up to her apartment complex and was just about to park in her designated parking spot when she spotted a man, dressed in all black, walking along side of her apartment. She focused in on him, as she watched to see what he was doing. Her heart dropped in her chest when she saw the man look into her living room window. Oh my God, someone is trying to break in my apartment. Bailey's eyes widened when she saw the pistol in the man's gloved hand. She was just about to back out of the parking lot when the man noticed Bailey's car and aimed his gun towards it. Bailey ducked, just as the bullet hit her side mirror.

She screamed, as she cut her wheel and placed her foot on the gas. Her car ran over the curb, as she attempted to get away. She swerved several times in an effort not to hit any of the parked cars. Her heart pounded in her chest and her hands shook so badly, she could hardly hold the steering wheel. She watched as the man got into his car and pulled out the parking lot after her.

"Shit, shit, shit. What the fuck is going on?" Bailey yelled as she floored the gas. She reached for her purse and grabbed out her phone.

"Siri, call Nakia," Bailey ordered.

The phone rung several times before it went to voicemail. "Fuck!" Bailey cussed, hanging up the phone. Looking up in her rearview mirror, she saw the man was right on her tail. Tears began to fall freely from her eyes as fear filled her entire body. Bailey picked up speed, as she tried to get as far away from the man as possible.

"Siri, call Anastasia."

"Hey Bailey, what's up?" Anastasia answered cheerfully.

"Anastasia, a man is following me, and he has a gun. Oh my God! I'm so scared Anastasia, I don't know what to do," Bailey cried.

"What? What do mean someone is following you? Who is it? Where are you?"

Bailey told Anastasia what happened when she pulled up to her apartment. "What if it's that man Nakia and I are supposed to testify against? The agent already told us the star witness was murdered in her home. Oh my God... he's going to kill me, Anastasia!" Bailey screamed frantically.

"Calm down, Bailey, and tell me where you are? Is there a police station close by?" Anastasia asked.

"I'm on my way to the police station now, please just stay on the phone with me until I get there."

"Oh, for sure I will. Do you really think it's that man? How does he know where you live?" Anastasia asked.

"I don't know, but like for real, who else could it be? Ain't nobody just gonna be coming to my house shooting at me. It's definitely him, or somebody he sent."

Just then, Bailey felt her car jerk as Raphael hit her from behind, causing her to scream out loud and almost drop her phone. She looked into her mirror, just as he hit her for a second time. She almost lost control of her car and had to ease off the gas a little bit and turn her wheel slightly to the left, in order not to crash.

"Bailey, what's going on? What was that?"

"He just crashed into the back of me, twice. I'm so scared, Anastasia, what should I do?"

"Oh my God, how close to you to the police station?" Anastasia asked.

"I'm still about a mile away. Anastasia, I hope I make it. No matter how fast I go, he's still right behind me."

"You're gonna make it, just calm down and keep driving. Don't look back, just keep driving, Bailey," Anastasia encouraged.

Keeping her tear-filled eyes on the road, Bailey drove as fast as she could down the street. She prayed that she could just make it inside the police station, because she knew she would be safe if she did. She didn't want to die; it was still so many things in the world she wanted to see. All she kept thinking about was how she should have never spoken with the police that day. Thinking she was doing something good for some teenage girls had ultimately turned out to be damn near fatal for her. God if you let me make it out of this, I promise you I will mind my own business from now on, Bailey prayed silently.

"I'm almost there, I can see it from where I am," Bailey voiced.

"Good, just keep driving. Have you talked to Nakia?" Anastasia asked.

"I called her right before I called you, but she didn't answer the phone. I pray she's okay."

"Yes, me too," Anastasia agreed.

"I'm here now, just pulled into the parking lot, and the car kept going. I'm gonna go inside and speak with the police," Bailey rushed off the phone and ran into the police station, trying to save her life.

Raphael cussed to himself as Bailey's car turned into the Garden City police station. He knew there was no way he could get her now, so instead, he kept driving. With it being dark and him being in all black, Raphael knew she wouldn't be able to give a positive description of him, however, he still needed to get as far away from the police station as possible. Raphael pulled up to his mother and father's house, placing the car he was driving into the garage before getting into his own car.

Now that Bailey had gone to the police, he would have to be extremely careful on how he went about things. He'd been in such a rush to get back home to Nakia that he'd moved sloppily and let his target get away. He knew his father wouldn't be pleased if he told him she was able to go to the police, so he didn't tell him. Instead, he got into his car and began to drive home.

Nakia walked into the house and placed the food on the kitchen counter. Raphael's car wasn't in the driveway, so Nakia knew he was still with his dad. Heading up to their room, she decided to take a bubble bath while she waited on him to return home. Although she was hungry, she didn't want to eat without Raphael, so she chose to wait.

Turning on the hot water, she added her bubbles before picking out a pair of pajamas to wear. Nakia lit a few candles and placed them around the tub before cutting the bathroom lights off. She stepped into the tub, sitting into the warm soothing water. She closed her eyes as she relaxed and let the scent of lavender invade her nostrils. She wasn't used to her house being this quiet, and she had to admit she kind of liked it. After an hour-long soak in the tub, Nakia got out and put on her pajamas. She just slid into her house shoes when she heard a glass break downstairs. Shaking her head, wondering what Raphael had broken, she called out to him. When he didn't answer, she put on her robe and walked out of their room.

"Raphael, baby, you, okay? What you down there breaking? I picked us up some Indian food for dinner. I hope you're ready to eat, because I'm starving," Nakia called out, as she walked towards the stairs.

An eerie feeling came over her when she got to the top of the stairs, and she felt as though something wasn't right. A chill crept down her spine, stopping her from walking down the stairs. Looking out over the huge window in her grand entry way, she looked over at the driveway. Her heart dropped when she noticed only her car was outside. Nakia's legs shook, and she thought they would give out on her and cause her to fall to the ground. Someone was in the house with her, and it wasn't Raphael.

She backed up slowly towards her room and heard more noises downstairs. She cussed to herself because she knew the person heard her calling for Raphael. Once she made it back to her room, she closed the door and went to grab her cell phone from her purse. Nakia cussed herself again when she realized her purse was downstairs on the kitchen counter next to the food. Her heart pounded in her chest as she looked around the room, looking for anything to use as a weapon. God, Raphael, where are you? Please just hurry and come home, Nakia begged. She knew if Raphael walked through the door, she would be safe, because he would protect her.

Nakia picked up the lamp from her nightstand, clutching it tightly in her hands. It wasn't much, but it was all Nakia had. To save her life and the life of her unborn child, she would beat the brains out of whoever walked through her bedroom door. With sweaty hands she held the lamp, as she watched her doorknob jiggle. She rocked back and forth, shaking in fear.

She had no idea what waited for her on the other side of that door, and her anxiety was through the roof. When the person on the other side realized the door was lock, they began kicking the door so hard, Nakia knew they would kick it off the hinges. Thinking quick on her feet, Nakia ran into the bathroom, locking herself inside just as her bedroom door was kicked open.

"You can't run from me, bitch... all you doing is making it worse on yourself. I don't like to work hard, and you making this real hard, bitch. I hurt my shoulder trying to get in this fuckin' room, now Imma fuck you up before I kill you," Nakia heard the voice call out.

Nakia shook in fear but remained quiet. She knew it was only a matter of time before he found her, but she didn't want to lead him to her. She listened closely as the man searched the bedroom looking for her. Sweat poured from under her arms as she awaited her fate. There was nowhere for her to go, so Nakia knew if she wanted to live, she would have to fight. She heard the man come to the bathroom door and try to turn the knob. Fuck, he found me, Nakia thought to herself, as the man kicked the door down instantly.

"Yeah bitch, there yo snitchin' ass go. You thought you could run from me huh? What you runnin' for? You was just runnin' to the police, now yo ass runnin' for yo life, huh bitch?" The man asked, as he took a few steps closer to Nakia.

"Please don't hurt me, I'm pregnant," Nakia pleaded.

Niko looked down at her stomach and laughed sinisterly. Leaping towards her, Niko placed his hands around Nakia's neck and began choking her. Nakia's eyes rolled into the back of her head as she attempted to breath. Realizing she still had the lamp in her hand, she hit Niko over the head with it as hard as she could, causing him to break the grip he had on her neck.

"Bitch, I know you didn't just hit me!" Niko roared, as he placed his hand up to the open gash on his head. With his free hand, he back-handed Nakia so hard, she fell onto the hard floor, landing on her stomach. She instantly screamed out, as pain shot through her body.

"Oh my God, my baby!" Nakia yelled out as she cradled her stomach in her hands.

She felt a pop, and the wetness began seeping through her thighs. *God, please just keep my baby safe, I don't care what happens to me, but please save my baby,* Nakia pleaded silently. She looked up at the man standing over her, just as he pulled his gun from his waistline and aimed it at her.

TO BE CONTINUED...

The State's Witness 2
Coming Soon

KEEP READING FOR A PREVIEW OF...

Ridin' For You
By Telia Teanna

CHAPTER ONE

"Shit, I gotta answer this." Zyair put his long-tattooed index finger to his lips, quietly shh-ing her.

McKenzie looked up at him with amused eyes and opened her mouth wider, taking more of his thick dick into her mouth. His lips parted and his hips slightly thrusted up into her mouth.

He was naked from the waist down. His onyx skin caused her mouth to water with the way that the sun shined through the large floor to ceiling windows of the condo he bought her recently.

"Wassup, baby?"

From her knees McKenzie's eyes shined bright with mischief as she watched her fuck buddy try not to moan while he was on the phone with his fiancée. She could hear her on the other side ask him where he was, so purposely gagged on his dick, making him inhale sharply.

"Oh shit," he mumbled under his breath, tangling a big hand in the expensive Peruvian bundles that he had bought her also.

"Nothin'. I'm just taking a shit."

McKenzie choked on his dick because she laughed. This nigga ain't shit. She was laughing on the inside. Only a dumb bitch would believe some shit like that. Niggas don't take shit outside their houses.

He bit his lip and nodded down at McKenzie, humor lighting up his normally empty eyes. He knew that she always got off on doing nasty shit to him while he was on the phone with his bitch.

He'd be a lying ass nigga if he said that he never planned some of the calls between them. Her pussy was soaking wet every time. Even at that moment he knew she was enjoying every moment of him being on the phone while she sucked him off. She was playing with that little wet pussy, and it only made him grow harder in her mouth.

"How was your day, babe?" He asked. He knew that if he asked, she was going to talk his ear off for the next twenty minutes before asking if he was paying attention.

"Weeeell, I went to the mall today, right?" He muted his mic and dropped it on the couch.

"I'm funny to you, huh?" McKenzie's bronze eyes met his almost black ones and winked at him, taking his long dick down her throat, swallowing him.

"Fuuuuuck," he moaned, sinking further into the couch and spreading his legs wider apart.

That trick right there was the very reason why he could never leave her ass alone. He couldn't imagine a life where he couldn't get his whole dick swallowed the way she did it. No other bitch had been able to do so, and he doubted that another bitch could.

"Mmmm," she moaned around his shaft when he tangled both his hands in her hair and thrusted in and out of her throat, moaning loudly.

That was another thing that was special about McKenzie, she was with whatever pleased him sexually. She basically let him use her as his personal fuck doll.

Yes, he had a whole girl at home that he was going to be marrying in just a few months, but there was no fucking way that he could exist in life without McKenzie's sex. She was the only one that could ever completely satiate him. And truthfully, he didn't care that he had a woman that worshipped the ground that he walked on at home.

The two could have made the perfect couple, but McKenzie didn't want to be tied down.

He groaned. "Fuck, I love this throat." He licked his lips and removed his hands from her head to let her breath.

The way his wet dick slid out of her throat and she looked up at him with "fuck me" eyes and for a second, he lost his train of thought and saw nothing but her.

"Better answer her." Her sultry voice broke him from his trance.

McKenzie chuckled and slapped his big black dick against her tongue. She loved the attention and intensity that he gave her when she was making him feel good. She didn't know why but she loved sucking Zyair's dick so much, that sometimes she'd meet up with him when he was out in the field just so that she could get a taste of him and hear him moan her name.

She was his fucking weakness and she knew it. It was one of the many perks of having a baller ass nigga like Zy. His fire ass pipe game was another perk.

Her favorite perk.

He picked up the phone and unmuted it. "What you say, babe?"

"I asked what kind of flowers did you think that we should get for the wedding?"

Her question immediately irritated him. He didn't fucking know, nor did he care. He was busy trying to buss a nut down his side bitch's throat.

"You know I don't knoooow-" he drew out the words at the exact moment McKenzie released his dick from her mouth, lifted his balls and one of his legs, and licked his gooch.

"What the heck are you doing?"

He couldn't mask the moans that left him as she teased the sensitive space between his anus and balls.

McKenzie laughed against his flesh when she heard his girl going off.

"You're with that bitch, aren't you?" She was livid.

McKenzie pulled away from him and laughed out loud.

"He is, hoe. Now get the fuck off the phone so I can finish eating our nigga's ass, bitch," she taunted her.

"Zyair! You just gonna-" He hung up the phone.

"You always gotta fuckin' start some shit, Kenzie. Why you ain't just be quiet?" He huffed annoyed. He didn't feel like arguing with his bitch when he got home.

"'Cause I ain't feel like it." She winked at him and lowered herself onto her hands and knees. "Now, scoot down."

She didn't dare reach out to pull him further off the couch so she could reach her designation easier, he always threw a fit when she did. He'd go off on a rant talking about him being a grown ass man and not to handle him like he was some kind of bitch.

"I'ma stop fuckin' with you one day, I swear." He adjusted himself on the couch and pulled his shirt off and lifted one foot onto the couch, giving her better access to his ass.

"Is you?" She teasingly flicked her tongue across his asshole, and watched it pucker in response.

"Hell nah." He groaned and grabbed her by the back of the head and pressed her face back into his ass.

His eyes rolled into the back of his head. The fact that she ate his ass was another reason he'd never leave her alone.

Before Zyair met McKenzie, he never let a bitch anywhere near his ass. He wasn't with that gay shit, but he soon learned that when it came to McKenzie, she had no boundaries. If she wanted to do something, she was going to do it, and whoever she was dealing with was going to like it. And after the first time she licked that spot and gave him a rim job, he was hooked.

Eating his ass is what got her the big ass condo with a stunning view, she was eating his ass in.

"Mmm, jack my dick, babe."

She did as he instructed and wrapped both of her hands around his length and stroked him while repeatedly swirling her tongue around his asshole. His sexy moans and groans made her pussy drip for him. She couldn't wait to feel him inside of her. One thing she absolutely loved was seeing Zyair's controlling ass, losing his shit as she sucked and fucked him the way only some type of sex demon could.

"Oh shit, I'm gonna blow." His hands reached around to cup around hers and jerk him faster.

McKenzie removed her tongue from his ass and wrapped her mouth around the head of his dick, anxiously waiting to taste him.

He groaned loudly and shot his load into her warm mouth. His toes curled, heart raced, and dick throbbed. She made him cum harder than any other bitch that he had ever fucked. His ass wasn't going anywhere.

After swallowing his load, she sexually licked her lips, smiling at the visual of Zyair in all of his black ass glory. Just scrumptious. He flashed her a boyish grin that reminded her of his youthful age. He was heavy in the streets, so it made him a lot older than what he was. That's what pressure from the streets did to a young nigga.

She fought her the urge to grin back, and instead straddled his lap. His phone rang and they both looked at it to see his girl calling again. He flipped the phone so she couldn't see the screen and muted it.

"Don't worry about the phone. Come put that pussy in my face." He slapped her ass and watched her every movement while she climbed onto his face, mounting his tongue with a long moan.

Zyair wasted no time, stroking her large clit with gentle flicks. McKenzie had a bigger clit than any woman that he had ever been with. He used to think that it was a little weird. It was like licking on a small gumball, but he eventually embraced it and grew to love it.

Because her clit was so big, she was a lot more sensitive than any other woman he'd been with. Whenever he was licking on it, it made her go crazy on the dick after. It also helped that he genuinely enjoyed tasting her, especially since he didn't eat women out. Not even his fiancée. McKenzie though? That was some cake he'd never turn down. He devoured it every time.

His phone rang again, and a sneaky grin spread across her face. She leaned forward to grab his phone and answered it, putting it on speaker.

"Will you stop callin'?"

"You're one bold bitch. You just love being slutted out by my man, don't you?"

McKenzie laughed, and then moaned loudly when he pinched her clit between his thick, dark lips. "'The fuckin' boldest. I ain't the one being slutted out, baby. Why the fuck you think this nigga can't stay away from me?"

Zyair moaned against her flesh, his dick hardening at her talking her shit. She was that bitch and couldn't nobody tell her shit. He loved it.

"Just because you're willing to let him treat you like some whore on the street doesn't mean anything, baby girl. At the end of the day, I'm the one that he put a ring on. This little thing y'all have going on won't last long. As soon as we're married, you'll be history, babe."

McKenzie laughed. *She's delusional.*

She hissed and ground her fat clit roughly against his wet tongue. She purposely moaned into the phone's mic.

"Girl, bye! You got that ring, because I didn't want it, bitch. Stop fucking playing with me. He's only your man because I let you have him, hoe!"

The more shit she talked, the harder he got, and the faster he ate her pussy. There was something so fucking sexy about his women fighting over him. He knew who his dick was rooting for, though.

"Yeah, you keep telling yourself that, sweetie. Will you put my man on the phone now?"

McKenzie moaned before responding. "Can't. He's eating and has his mouth full."

Zyair met her bronze eyes. She saw nothing but pure and unadulterated lust staring back at her. She grinned down at him.

He got off on her talking shit to his girl just as much as she did. She always knew just what he liked and how to help him take his orgasms to the next level.

"I'm gonna whoop your ass when I see you."

"I'm waiting hoe. You know where I be at." And with that, McKenzie hung up the phone and brushed one of her hands down the fade of his head.

Zyair gave her clit a few firm strokes with the tip of his tongue, and she imploded on his face.

"Why you so mean to my girl, Ken?" He asked when he unattached his lips from her pussy and licked and sucked the inside of her thighs.

"Why you let me be mean to your girl, Zy?" It was a legitimate question.

"Don't try to turn your fucked up-ness around on me."

"Ain't nobody doing shit. Every time you come around here wanting me to fuck and suck on you, your bitch wants to come starting shit with me. So, you damn right I'm mean to that bitch. The fuck you think I am, Zy?"

Her toffee skin flushed red, a sign that she was getting upset. He got up from his seated position and pushed her onto her back and settled himself between her legs, lining his thick dick up at her entrance.

"You right. Imma check her when I get home." He rubbed the head of his dick teasingly back and forth across that juicy clit of hers.

"You better. I'd hate to have to cut you off." She threatened through a moan, her pussy leaking in anticipation for him to fill her.

"You gone cut me off?" He slowly sank into her. She was so tight, wet, and warm that he had to throw his head back and really enjoy the feel of what he was convinced to be the best pussy in the world. That tight muthafucka made him feel like he was the luckiest nigga in the world to be blessed with such a wonderful experience.

"I will if I have to." She moaned and used her thumb to thrum her clit.

He pushed her hand away and replaced it with his own and caught on to a rhythm and slowly long stroked her. He wanted her to feel every inch of his big dick and remember why she couldn't stop fucking him just as much as he wouldn't stop fucking her.

"Yeah? You don't want me to put this dick in your stomach no more?"

She said nothing, so he pulled completely out of her and then slammed back into her roughly. "Huh?"

"No," she said through a moan.

Zyair rolled his eyes and slapped her inner thigh. "You fulla shit, but okay."

He pulled out of her and stood to his feet. Smirking down at her and picking her up, he threw her over his shoulder and walked out to the balcony. The sun was starting to set, and the heat of the day was finally starting to cool down.

McKenzie giggled as she slumped over his shoulder. She didn't know why, but his ass loved tossing her around and she let him.

They were both butt ass naked as he rested her on her feet to look out at the amazing view of the city, at that time. She had neighbors that only needed to look out of their windows to see them, but they didn't give a fuck. They've fucked for audiences before.

Kenzie took a deep breath amazed at the view every time she was out there. She was grateful for it. Her hands gripped the iron railing, and her lips parted when she felt the heat of his body enveloped her. One of his hands grabbed her hip, making her arch her back, and his other hand gripped his dick, as he fed it into her pussy.

Her body melted into him as soon as he entered her. He rested his face into the crook of her neck, holding her closely. The sounds of his moans in her ear making her wetter with every long, slow stroke.

"You like the view, baby?" He was curious.

He had been doing some house shopping with Kristina when he saw it. His fiancée didn't want any kids, so she wanted to move into a condo.

When they viewed it together, Kristina had fallen head over heels for the property. It was lavish, in a great area with a great view. Truly fit for a queen.

Too bad she wasn't the queen he felt was worthy enough of it.

As soon as he stepped inside and saw the large open concept, updated appliances, and the balcony, he knew that he was going to cop it for McKenzie. He knew that she was going to love it, and she did. She sucked his dick and ate his ass extra nastily the night he picked her up and surprised her with it.

"I love it, Zyair. Thank you." She turned her head so that she could kiss him.

He thrusted into her harder, making her moan every time he hit bottom.

"The world is yours, baby." And she believed him.

She knew that if she asked him for anything, he wouldn't hesitate to give it to her. If she called, he came running. When it came down to it, Zyair was the most consistent and reliable person in her life.

"A nigga just wishes that he was able to wake up in this bitch with you every morning and slide in this pussy." His hand drifted between her legs, thrumming her clit again.

McKenzie clutched the railing tighter and moaned. "You 'bout to marry a whole different woman, Zy."

He pumped into her harder, applying pressure to both her g-spot and her mental. "Whose fault is that?"

"Not mine!" She tried to pull away from him, but instead he pushed her into the railing and forcefully bent her over it. Her eyes widened and her heart raced in her chest as she looked at the large jagged edges of rocks fifteen feet below.

Zyair grabbed the railing, trapping her so that he could pound hard and fast into her. "Say the word, Kenz. Say it and I swear to God, I'll throw that bitch out like a dirty dish rag."

Her eyes rolled into the back of her head. He was hitting just the right spot that had her squirting all over his dick with each stroke. She didn't answer him just focused on how good he was making her feel.

"Look at this pussy wetting me up. You don't wanna wake up and go to sleep like this, Kenz? You don't want this?" He grabbed her around the throat and pulled her up so that her back was touching his chest.

She looked out at the view, and watched the sun set and all the city lights turn on in the distance as it began to darken. It was literally the most beautiful, erotic, and dare she say romantic thing she had experienced in her life. Tears welled in her eyes as she felt an orgasm swirling around in her gut, making her body tremble hard against him.

He had managed to get into her head, and she was fighting hard to not go there with him. She hated when he brought up them becoming more than what they were. She couldn't understand why he just couldn't keep things as they were.

"You don't want us, McKenzie?" His voice broke in the middle of his sentence.

"I'm cumming." Her words came out in a rush and through a moan as she let go.

Her orgasm prompted his and he released deep inside of her with a loud groan.

The two took a few moments to catch their breaths.

"Why you don't wanna be with me, McKenzie? Why am I never good enough for you?" He pulled out of her and took a few steps back.

McKenzie remained in the same position against the balcony railing. She stared blankly out at the view in front of her, tears freely streaming down her face. She remained quiet.

After a minute or two of silence, Zyair shook his head and turned to go back inside and put his clothes on. He knew that she wasn't going to answer him. She never did when he brought it up. And every time he did, his heart broke a little bit more each time.

He took his time showering and dressing. He was putting his Rolex back on his wrist when he emerged from her bedroom. McKenzie was on the couch nursing a drink, the sounds of H.E.R. playing softly from the speakers built into the ceiling throughout the place.

She was in a satin robe with her toffee legs tucked beneath her. He wanted nothing more than to just stay and be with her. They didn't even have to fuck all night like they normally did. He just wanted to be held by her, while they went back and forth roasting each other.

But he needed to go. His feelings were hurt, and he didn't want her to know it. Shit, he brought it on himself. He knew that she wouldn't give him a real answer as to why she didn't want to be exclusively his. It never stopped him from asking in hopes that he had somehow proved that he was worthy of her heart.

He made his way over to the couch where he had left his phone. The two of them locked eyes when he neared her. She held his phone out for him to take.

"You're more than enough, Zyair. Always have been." Her voice was horse from crying.

"Then what's the problem?" He was genuinely confused.

She diverted her eyes and he took a seat next to her on the couch and clasped his hands together.

"I'm the one who isn't good enough, Zy. Kristina though? She's good for you. Nice, gorgeous, intelligent, all of that. I don't have shit to offer you but ass."

In the two years he and McKenzie had been fucking around, he'd never heard her so sad and serious. He hated that she felt that way and was comparing herself to his girl when there was no need.

It also didn't sit well with him that she kept downplaying herself. He had never known her to be the insecure type, but that's exactly how she sounded in that moment and he felt guilty for it.

"That's not true," he protested.

She rolled her eyes and took a sip of her henny and coke. "It is, but okay. We don't even know each other like that and you talking about moving in here together."

His head jerked back. "Woah, we been fuckin' for two years, Kenz. How the hell do we not know each other? We ain't strangers, nigga."

"Exactly! We been fuckin'. That's it! We know nothing about each other outside of how we like to have sex."

His face was screwed up as he tried to process what she was saying. "That's bullshit."

She sighed and ran her fingers through her bundles. "What's my last name, Zyair?"

Silence.

She took another sip of her drink. "When's my birthday?"

"We celebrated your birthday together this year."

"Okay?" She raised an eyebrow at him and shifted so that she could look at him directly. "You should know when it is then, right?"

Damn. He had to think back and make a guess. "Uh, it's in March, right?" He scratched his head.

"No. You get my point, yet?"

He sighed and ran a hand down his face. "No. I never remember shit like that. That typa shit ain't important."

"That's why more will never be able to become of us, Zyair. That kind of shit is important to me. I don't wanna commit to you and then be disappointed that it's not all sugar and rainbows. There's a whole lot of shit that comes with fuckin' with a nigga like you. Being deemed yours in a city that you run will force me to be trapped in a bubble for many different reasons, none of which I'd care to experience."

"You know you've always been safe with me, McKenzie." That was a concern that he heard from women that he was involved with. It was a concern that Kristina constantly brought up to him when she tried to convince him to get out of the dope game and go legit.

His career of choice was in a dangerous industry. Niggas wanted his head everywhere he went and were willing to hurt anyone attached to him. The women he was with always wanted the benefits, but then got scared and ran when the risks got too risky. He thought that McKenzie was different and that she would be able to handle what came with his lifestyle. He was quickly becoming disappointed to know that everything that he had perceived her to be was the exact opposite.

"I'm not worried about street shit. I tote pistols too, nigga. I ain't never feared death. Six months ago, you proposed to me, and I said no. I didn't think you were ready for marriage. I still don't think you're ready. I don't even think that you are the marriage type at all. And you proved it to me when two months after turning you down, I look on fucking Instagram and see some preppy bitch with the ring you tried to give me on her finger, posted on your page."

She paused to calm herself down. Her voice was strained as she spoke, her emotions getting the best of her. He sat quietly, mentally kicking his own ass for the dumb shit that he had done.

"You like drama, Zyair. Cool, if that's what you want to do, fine. I get off on arguing and showing my ass in front of your bitches sometimes, too. It's been fun. But I'm damn near thirty, this shit is getting old. My feelings are involved, and honestly, you giving that bitch my ring, hurt like hell.

"Being with you will mean that everybody knows that I'm yours. Therefore making me off limits, cause the niggas in this city is mad pussy and never go against you. And at the same time, you can still, and more than likely will still be out in the streets doing you. I'm not that dumb of a bitch, Zyair. If we go there, I know for a fact that I will lose you the same damn way I got you. That's how karma works."

She finished off the rest of her drink.

He sighed and sat back against the couch, thinking. She had a few points. He wanted to tell her that she had everything wrong but figured that he should just keep it to himself until they were more emotionally under control.

"I'm just gonna go." He had a whole lot that he wanted to say, but the timing was off.

They needed some time apart, so he was going to give her that. She was nodding her head when he stood up. Her eyes were staring blankly out of the living room window, and she stayed in that position until she heard the front door close, and finally, she let the tears fall down her face.

Coming Soon
January 2023

OTHER BOOKS BY

URBAN AINT DEAD

Tales 4rm Da Dale

By **Elijah R. Freeman**

The Hottest Summer Ever

By **Elijah R. Freeman**

Despite The Odds

By **Juhnell Morgan**

The Swipe

By **Toōla**

Hittaz 1 & 2

By **Lou Garden Price, Sr**

Good Girls Gone Rogue

By **Manny Black**

COMING SOON FROM

URBAN AINT DEAD

The Hottest Summer Ever 2
By **Elijah R. Freeman**

THE G-CODE
By **Elijah R. Freeman**

How To Publish A Book From Prison
By **Elijah R. Freeman**

Tales 4rm Da Dale 2
By **Elijah R. Freeman**

Ridin' For You
By **Telia Teanna**

Hittaz 3
By **Lou Garden Price, Sr.**

The State's Witness 2
By **Kyiris Ashley**

The Swipe 2
By **Toōla**

A Setup For Revenge
By **Ashley Williams**

Good Girl Gone Rogue 2
By **Manny Black**

Charge It To The Game
By **Nai**

Despite The Odds 2
By **Juhnell Morgan**

BOOKS BY

URBAN AINT DEAD's C.E.O

Elijah R. Freeman

Triggadale 1, 2 & 3

Tales 4rm Da Dale

The Hottest Summer Ever

Murda Was The Case 1 & 2

Follow

Elijah R. Freeman

On Social Media

FB: Elijah R. Freeman

IG: @the_future_of_urban_fiction

Made in United States
Troutdale, OR
11/22/2023

14832734R00096